Editing by: Dragonfly Editing

Published by Cauldron Press

info@cauldronpress.online

Visit www.ansage.ca

AETHERQUEEN

The AetherBorn Saga, Book 2

A. N. SAGE

CAULDRON
PRESS

"Uneasy lies the head that wears a crown."
-William Shakespeare

CHAPTER 1
CLOAKED FIGURES IN THE DARK

T he room was pure darkness, the kind of dark that starless nights are made of. There was a chill in the air and Ruby could feel her breath turn to mist as she gasped for air. She was trying to move but something was holding her back, keeping her hands restrained. What was that? She could feel the cold, rough edges of it rubbing against her wrists as she wiggled, attempting to break free, without much luck.

She tried to scream but there was no sound, and even if she could manage to yell out, she was certain there was nobody who could help her. She was alone in this. Ruby closed her eyes and thought of Liam. His green eyes watching her every move, the warmth of his hands when he touched hers, the smile that made her forget everyone else in the room. Where was he? Why was he not rushing to her side as he had done so many times before?

There was a scratching sound that jarred her back to the room. Her eyes blinked madly as they tried to adjust to the dark. Something was wrong. She could feel it. She wasn't alone at all. The darkness moved around her, shifting focus and changing shape. It slowly swirled into chaotic figures, dancing a waltz in front of her unbelieving eyes.

Ruby struggled harder against her restraints, she needed to get out of here. As her gaze moved around the room, she could see that it wasn't darkness that filled the room, instead, she was surrounded by nightly figures, standing close enough to one another that no sliver of light could get through. She tried to make out their faces but it was as if they had none. Underneath their clothing, black fog moved, mimicking the movements of a human being.

The scratching intensified. As it grew louder, Ruby's attention shifted to the back of the room. One of the figures swayed to the side letting a light shine through. The illumination was growing slowly, filling the room to the edges. She should have been happy to be able to see again, but something did not feel right. Ruby could feel the anger emanating from it, trying to swallow her whole.

She gave one last push forward, ripping the restraints off her. Her hands intertwined as she concentrated, shooting a fireball through the dark crowd. The fire moved through them, parting them like opening gates. Ruby pushed her way through, running towards a *window on the other side of the room. With her hands against it, she clumsily pawed at the frame to find a lock, catching a glimpse of the outside. It was bright, too bright for this hour of the night. Her eyes studied the light, trying to make sense of it.*

When her vision finally came into focus, she was horrified. She stumbled backwards, a scream forming on the edges of her lips.

In front her eyes, the training center was burning in a blaze that she knew not one Elemental could survive.

RUBY WOKE UP IN A SWEAT, clutching the Onyx necklace with both hands and panting for breath. She reached over, hoping Liam would be beside her so she could burrow herself into his arms for the comfort she so badly needed right now. Her hands cradled the cold pillow instead. Of all the times to spend the night alone, why did it have to be on the day her visions decided to come back? She closed her eyes, taking solace in the fact that she would see him again in just a few hours.

It was just a dream, she thought. But her eyes spent the rest of the night wide open, watching for fogged figures in the dark.

3

CHAPTER 2
ENJOY YOUR DAY, MY QUEEN

The training center was buzzing with chatter. Ever since they opened their doors to the rest of the Elementals, it was full to the brim with people coming in and out at all hours. There were people bursting the seams of each room. Some were training, some attended classes, others just came by to catch up with new friends. Seeing so many people here made Ruby remember her own classes. She was nowhere near ready to go back to school in the fall. Something about it seemed so unimportant now, compared to everything she had to deal with lately.

She walked the halls taking it all in. She still couldn't believe that she was responsible for all of these people. With the Water House sword piece missing and there still not being any clues as to its whereabouts, the pressure of being an AetherBorn was starting to wear her down. Each day that went by without answers felt like a personal failure to her. She knew that she had support in Liam and the elders but at the end of the day, she'd signed up to keep them safe and she still did not feel like she was strong enough for the job. It was bad enough that Elena had to do everything but hold her hand when Ruby was dividing the sword into five pieces but now it seemed their decision to do so may have brought a thief into the den. After the elders had agreed on the peace treaty, she was certain that breaking the sword apart was the best solution. Giving each house a piece of the metal and their rightful stone so they would be forced to work together. It took many tries to separate the tough metal and almost all of her energy. Even with Elena's soothing voice guiding her every step of the way, she took days to form a strong enough connection to the sword that would allow her to shatter it. It was as though it didn't want to be broken. Ruby had woken up for many mornings after wondering if it was trying to warn her somehow. If she was only smart enough to take the warning.

Her footsteps quickened as she made her way past the lunchroom towards the greenhouse. She hadn't seen Liam yet this morning and had a feeling she would find him there, taking solace amidst the greenery. It was his favorite place in the center, after all.

Dodging a few kids running down the hall, her eyes brightened at the sight of him. His hair a perfect mess, leaning against the glass wall of the greenhouse. His gaze landed on her, and a smile curled on his lips.

She ran towards him, jumping into his arms as he scooped her up into a tight hug. His strong arms pressed her close, almost lifting her in the air. Ruby grabbed hold of his face, pulling him into her, his burning lips against hers felt like home. They stayed there, in the middle of the hallway, intertwined, smiling like two fools without a care in the world.

"So, you guys going to say hello or just make us gag the whole day?"

Ruby jumped back, just now noticing Zag and his sister Leah standing next to them. She tried to bury her flushed cheeks in the loose strands of her hair but the damage was already done. Zag was hunched over, emulating the act of throwing up that made Leah howl with laughter.

"Sorry, guys. Didn't see you there." She said nervously, and brushed her hair back into place. She could see Liam smiling from the corner of her eye, clearly proud of his distracting quality.

"Right. Whatever you say, princess." Zag elbowed Liam's side and chuckled, still amused at his own jokes. "Have you had coffee yet? I just put a pot on in the kitchen."

Liam's fingers wrapped around hers, pulling her towards the lunch room. "I could use another cup for sure."

As they made their way over, Leah was her usual chatterbox. She had a million questions about the sword piece and what symbols Ruby saw when they found it missing. Her bright red, pixie hair bounced as she frolicked down the hall with them.

"What did they look like? Are you sure they're not Elemental? What are we going to do next?"

Ruby didn't know which question to answer first. She loved Leah's bubbly personality but after her vision last night, she thought it best not to talk about the sword until she had a chance to brief the elders on what she saw. No point causing panic just yet. "Let's just get a coffee in us first. I think we all need a break from talking about the sword."

"Speak for yourself!" Zag yelled out, steps ahead of them now, "Leah and I have already started going over possible suspects."

Of course, they have, she thought. The two of them were like two Elemental detectives. Much too interested in mysteries and drama. Ruby wished she shared their enthusiasm for this, but all she could think of was the danger it presented. Everything she had fought so hard to achieve could be gone in seconds if an Elemental decided to go rogue and abandon the peace treaty.

"Guys, give her a minute to breathe, huh? She hasn't even had a chance to get in and you're already all over her." Liam's tone suggested he was as done with talking about this as she was.

"Ugh, fine. But don't think I don't have more questions for you. This is better than TV!" Leah flipped her short hair to the side and ran ahead into the kitchen.

"Sorry about them." Liam smiled when they were finally alone, "how was your night with Shaylah last night? Did you guys catch up?"

"Sort of. All she wanted to talk about is you, to be honest."

"Oh yeah? I always liked that Shaylah," he smirked. "And what did you tell her, exactly?"

"Oh, you know, that you're kind of boring, not the best to look at, not really my type at all." Ruby laughed as she said the last part, knowing full well that he was as much her type as anyone could get. In fact, she hadn't even known she had a type, before Liam. He would certainly be a tough act to follow.

"So, that's how it's going to be, huh? Well, I guess I'll just go on my way then. Enjoy your day, my queen."

He turned around and pretended to walk away. Ruby's hand grabbed hold of his sweatshirt, spinning him back around and pulling him towards her. She placed her finger on his lips and smiled. "You know you're stuck with me, right?"

"Stuck is not how I see it at all," His arm swept around her and pushed her towards the lunch room doors, "come on, let's get that coffee to go. I told Alice we'd come see her as soon as you get in this morning."

"Liam?"

"What's up? You all right?"

"Not exactly. I had a vision last night."

"What? Why didn't you lead with that? You haven't had a vision since the treaty! What was it?"

Ruby wanted to grab his arm and get out of there. To leave the center and get out of Westerlake entirely. She hated having this much responsibility, but more than that, she hated not being able to just have a normal relationship with a boy she cared about more than anyone. To go on dates, to daydream about him, to plan a life together. None of that could happen now. At least not until they figured out who stole the sword piece and how to get it back.

"Let's just go see Alice. She should probably hear about this, too," she said, and squeezed his hand. There was no running away from her visions, not when all of the Elementals counted on her to keep them safe.

CHAPTER 3
WE'RE GETTING CLOSE

"I hear you didn't get much sleep last night." Jake noted when they walked into the library. News in the center seemed to travel faster than a cheetah chasing prey.

"Yeah. It was definitely..." she thought for a moment, trying not to escalate the issue, "unsettling."

It'd been a few months now since the awkward encounter she'd had with Jake, before the peace treaty. His proclamation of love put a wedge between them that had only worsened when Ruby used it to gain access to the sword. She knew it would be a long time until they could get back to the friendship they'd once shared, but something felt off about him lately. Ruby was used to him acting strange around her and Liam, though they kept their public affections to a minimum when he was around. In the last few weeks, however, his distaste for them was much more obvious. It was as if he was trying to purposefully put a wedge between them.

"Surprised Liam wasn't there to help you through it," he chuckled.

Right on cue, she thought. Her hair fell in her face and she was grateful when it covered her eyes, which were glowing with anger right about now. "It was girls' night, with Shaylah."

It wasn't long until Liam's hand brushed against her lower back, he could likely hear the banter from across the room and ran to her rescue. She knew she had Jake handled, but was thankful for the distraction. There was no need to cause a scene when there were bigger issues to discuss. She let Liam lead her towards the head of the table in the center of the library, and settled into a cozy position with her feet tucked under her, avoiding Jake's eyeroll as she passed.

Minutes after, there was a rustle at the door and Alice made her way to the table. "Sorry I'm running a bit behind this morning, everyone. The younger kids needed some help with their fireballs in training."

"No worries. Are Harvey and Myriam joining us?" Ruby was really hoping to get all the elders together for this.

"I'm afraid not. They're still trying to get through some research on the symbols. We're close to pinpointing their origin so I thought it best to leave them to it. You know how they get when they're researching."

Alice's smile made Ruby bounce in a giggle. She knew exactly how they got when they're busy, mumbling to themselves and dancing around each other in circles. It was quite a sight to take in. "I think Elena and Cyril are on their..."

The door swung open and two bodyguards marched into the room.

These two never miss a good entrance, she thought and watched Cyril escort Elena to the table.

Ruby studied their faces as they made their way to the table. They were still as regal as always but ever since Ruby took over as the head of the Elementals, there was more humility in their behavior than she ever expected to see. They were definitely trying to keep the peace, making Ruby wonder if it was just a cover up. Maybe it was one of them that had arranged for the theft of the Water house sword piece? Elena was likely not involved, but she could put nothing past Cyril. Even months later, she still had not forgiven him for what he did to Liam before her travel back in time.

"Hello, everyone. I trust you all had a good night?" Elena said, studying Ruby's face intently. "Any news on those symbols?"

"Not yet. But we're getting close, Harvey and Myriam should have something for us soon." Ruby shifted her weight, sitting up taller and showing a more prominent position, "speaking of good nights, yesterday, I had a vision. One I think we need to discuss as a team."

"Oh?" Cyril's eyebrows rose in suspicion. He darted a look at Jake who shook his head to indicate he was just as in the dark as everyone else here.

"I'm not sure what it means yet, so I don't want anyone to worry."

"Ruby, you understand we're going to worry every time you have a vision?"

"I know, Elena. Which is why I think it's best we go over every detail. Maybe there is something I missed that someone here can catch."

As if on instinct, she reached for Liam's hand. A swarm of butterflies knotted her stomach but she wasn't sure whether it was the excitement of being near him or the nervousness of retelling her vision. With her feet planted firmly on the ground, she started at the beginning.

CHAPTER 4

LESS OBVIOUS

"Does anyone else think this is too coincidental?" Elena said, "the treaty has only been in place for a few short months, a sword piece has gone missing, and now you have a threatening vision?"

She wasn't wrong, it was all much too close for comfort for Ruby. She had just started to gain the trust of the four houses and it felt like a snowball of bad luck was heading her way. Ruby had never been one to be prone to superstition, but she was starting to feel like something was against her succeeding in her new role.

"Well, at least we can rule out an Elemental from the theft."

"How do you figure, Cyril?" Ruby's eyes studied his expression. She tried to see if he meant his words or was just using her vision as a way to deflect blame. "There was nothing in my vision that even hinted at the sword." She stated matter of factly, trying to understand his reasoning to tie her vision to the theft.

"No, but if it was an Elemental that stole it, why would you get a vision of this center being in danger? It doesn't work in anyone's favor to set it on fire. Their own people would be trapped inside."

He had a point. Something about the vision didn't make sense to Ruby. The fogged figures, the darkness within them, nothing about their presence felt Elemental.

"Unless they had time to get their people out." Alice noted, "what do you think, Liam? You've been pretty quiet so far."

"Honestly, right now I'm just wondering how Ruby is feeling." His eyes were trained on her face and she could see Jake roll his eyes again in the background. If he didn't stop this, one of these days she'd have to slap those eyes right out of their sockets. "I don't think it's good for you to stay alone right now."

Her face started to heat up at Liam's words. She didn't appreciate being treated like someone who needed protection. If she was going to be a leader, she needed to show strength and his constant worrying was not helping. "I'm fine. It's not me you should be worried about."

Ruby pushed up from the table and leaned in closer to the group, shaking off Liam's hand in the process.

"There is a good chance we're taking this vision much too literally. The fire did not have to be an actual fire. So far, my visions have always been less obvious," she glanced at Jake, remembering the vision she had of him drowning, "it could just have meant that the Elementals are in danger. We don't know how for sure."

"Either way, we need to get ahead of this," Elena was looking directly at Ruby now, "we're not any closer to finding out what the symbols mean." Her stare burnt through Ruby, making her feel like she was starting to lose her breath. She could feel the pressure of having to come up with an idea drop like an anvil on her head.

Think of something clever to say, she thought but her mouth had a different plan. "Right," she uttered.

"Well, those symbols could have meant nothing. They could have just been a distraction."

"That was no distraction, Cyril. You weren't there. Those symbols had power, power I haven't felt before." Ruby uncrossed her arms and pushed two fists into the table, "it was the same power I felt in my vision. Something dark, unlike anything I've seen in this center or from any interaction with Elementals."

There was a moment of complete silence in the room. It was as though everyone was thinking carefully of the next words they wanted to use. Picking at them with a fork like a kid does with Brussels sprouts before pushing the plate away. Alice was the first to speak up, "Ruby, I know you don't want to hear it, but I think maybe Liam is right. Maybe it's best if you moved back into the facility for a little while. Just until we figure out what the vision meant."

"Look, I appreciate the concern, I really do. I don't want anyone to worry and it would be easier not having to commute every day to get here."

"Great! So, it's settled! We can go get your things tonight," Liam's face lit up.

"Not tonight, Liam. I can't just leave in the middle of the night without Shay getting suspicious. If I'm going to move back here, you need to give me time to break the news to my roommate before she calls the cops thinking I'm joining a cult," she could see the disappointment in his eyes. She leaned in closer to him, pressing her lips to his ear in a whisper, "Come on, the last thing you want to do on our date tonight is watch me pack. I can think of a few other things we could be doing."

"Hello? Still in a meeting here," Jake bellowed.

"Sorry. It's fine, we'll figure it all out. Right now, what we need to worry about most of all is getting a lead on those symbols and figuring out who took the sword piece. We can't afford to waste time on anything but that."

Ruby got up from the table, giving Liam a look that

implied she was more than ready to leave. She couldn't wait to get out of that room. Away from Jake's sarcastic jabs and Cyril's murderous face. But mostly, away from her own responsibilities.

"MIND if I steal you away for a minute?" Alice caught up with them on the way out. Her face was unreadable, there was not a trace of the usual tranquility it always possessed.

"Sure!" she reached over and gave Liam a kiss on the cheek, "I'll catch up with you, okay?"

When he walked off out of sight, she followed Alice around the corner. "Is everything all right?"

"Yes, of course. I just wanted to see how you're doing."

"Oh. I mean, I'm okay. A little tired but okay." She tried to put on her brightest smile, but it came out flat and uneventful.

"Ruby, I hope you don't mind me offering you some advice." Alice stopped and reached for her hand. Her palms were as warm as Liam's, a common trait for Fire Elementals. "I understand your need to have your own space, to not be surrounded by all of this daily."

"But?"

Alice let out a chuckle. "There's always a 'but' isn't there?"

"Usually," she grimaced.

"I do agree with Liam about you not being alone right now."

"I'm not alone there. I have Shaylah."

"Ruby, honey. You know I'm always on your side, right? In fact, I pretty much think of you as a daughter, at this point." She looked down at her feet and Ruby's heart broke a little. Alice had never had children of her own and hearing those words made her wonder if she regretted it. "So, I would never make you do anything that you're not comfortable with." She continued.

"I feel another 'but' coming on..."

"You're a leader now, Ruby. A queen really. I never wished for you to have to be burdened with this, but it's where we are now. Shaylah is great, but your priority needs to be here. At least until we can understand if there is a threat to the sword. Or against you."

Ruby's chest tightened. She knew there wasn't much of a choice, but she was starting to regret taking on the responsibility of guarding the sword in the first place. Wasn't a proper leader supposed to be able to make her own decisions? At least about where she sleeps at night? Alice was only saying what everyone around her was thinking, but she still didn't like the idea that her world was out of her own control. "I'll think about it."

"That's great!" Alice reached over and gave her a

hug, "it'll be great to get to spend some more time with you!

"Oh, and have fun on your date tonight!" She looked over her shoulder and winked, leaving Ruby standing alone, wondering how she was going to get out of leaving the apartment she loved.

CHAPTER 5
SO STRONG AND SO WEAK

Her favorite nights with Liam were always the simplest ones. Ruby often listened to Shaylah recount her extravagant dates in over the top restaurants, theatre visits, and once, even a hot air balloon ride. Each time her friend's eyes lit up from a different adventure, Ruby couldn't help but think about how different they were. She could not imagine wanting to ride up thousands of feet in the air with Liam, mostly because their Elemental life was already adventurous enough.

Tonight, Ruby needed simplicity more than anything. It took her a bit to persuade Liam to cancel their dinner reservations and just order in and watch a movie. He was convinced she needed a break from the center, but Ruby wanted nothing more than to spend time with him in his room, with enough sushi to feed a small country, and a cheesy flick on. With her friend-ship with Jake on hold, she managed to coerce Liam into several nights of B-rated horror movies, and though he wasn't as impressed with them as she was, she knew she'd wear him down sooner or later. Tonight's special was a particularly terrible rendition of the Titanic, told from the point of view a zombie, and she couldn't help but laugh with every questioning look Liam shot her way throughout.

"I seriously will never understand where you store all that food," he joked watching her polish off a third dynamite roll, "it must be some AetherBorn magic."

"Yeah, ok. This coming from the guy who can liter-ally eat two steaks in a row and still be hungry."

"That was one time. And we were training!"

She pressed her back against his chest, getting comfortable on the bed. His heartbeat quickened as it often did and she could feel her own match the pace. The excitement of being near him always surprised her. They'd been spending almost every day together and she was sure that at some point it would subside, but her now numb legs chose to differ. He was absolutely magnetic.

"Hey, Rue. Can I ask you a question?"

"It's about the vision, isn't it?" she asked, watching his brows furrow. "Fine, but I don't want to spend all night talking about it. This is supposed to be our night off and they're just about to eat the captain!" Her finger pointed at the screen with excitement.

"I know. I just worry about you. You're taking on a lot here."

"I get that you're worried, but at some point, I really need you to relax a little," Ruby felt him stiffen under her weight, "no offence."

"Right. That's a little easier said than done, I'm afraid."

"And why's that, exactly?"

"You know why. I'll never stop worrying. I'm sorry, but that's just not going to happen."

"It's ok to worry. I worry about you, too. Quite a bit, actually. But you need to trust that I can do this," she was starting to get upset with him, "I am an AetherBorn after all. A leader, by right."

His face tightened. She knew how much he hated the responsibility she chose to bear when she accepted her role in the treaty. It was probably difficult for him to understand why someone would take in so much of their world so quickly. A part of her knew that he could never really understand it. After all, she never told him about what she saw the night of the treaty, before she travelled back in time. How could she ever explain what it felt like to watch him die?

Liam put his palm to her cheek, squeezing the back of her head slightly towards him. As she leaned into him, she knew the conversation was over, the last thing either of them wanted to do was talk. She twisted her body around so she could bury herself in his arms, pulling him in, pressing the air between them away. Her voice trapped in her throat as his tongue parted her lips lightly. No one else could make her feel so strong and so weak at the same time.

CHAPTER 6
UNWIND A LITTLE

It was almost midnight by the time Liam walked her home. Her face was still flushed from the evening and she tried to make as little noise as possible opening the creaky door of her apartment. She barely had time to take her shoes off when she heard Shaylah's loud yelp from the living room.

"Fish! Get your skinny butt in here and dish!" her friend shouted, eager to hear about her date.

"Geez, Shay. Shouldn't you be in bed already?"

She walked over to the couch and plopped herself down in exhaustion. Shaylah's questioning stare made her uncomfortable. She quickly rearranged her hair knowing full well it was likely a shambled mess at this point.

"So? How was your night?" Shaylah stretched the last word playfully.

"It was fine. Just some takeout and a movie."

"Yeah. Ok. How much of the movie did you actually see?"

"The whole thing. Pretty much."

Shaylah stretched her foot to nudge her. Her eyes gleaming mischievously, waiting for details. "That's doubtful."

"Are you going to do this every time I see him? It's been, like, months now."

"Just until you stop having that dumb smile on your face. You're obsessed, Fish." She wasn't wrong, Ruby had the worst poker face when it came to her feelings for Liam. "So, did anything new happen or are we still playing the bases?"

"Calm down. It was just a regular date. No need to break out the champagne."

"Honestly, Rue," Shay said, clearly disappointed, "what is the hold up? Have you seen this guy? He's gorgeous!"

Ruby sat up a bit, pulling her sweatshirt closer to herself. Shaylah wasn't wrong, she didn't know what she was waiting for. The right moment perhaps? It seemed difficult to find the right moment when in the back of her mind all she could think about was how to save the Elementals. She loved being with Liam but she could never let herself truly relax, there was too much at stake right now.

"He is pretty stunning, isn't he?" She smiled.

"Yeah, I'd say so. I mean if I was you..."

"We all know what you would do if you were me, Shay."

"Rude! I just meant that maybe you should have some fun for a change. All you've been doing is working on this little school project with him, with a few dates here and there. Don't you just want to unwind a little?"

You have no idea! Ruby thought. The only thing she wanted was to have a normal relationship with Liam. Unfortunately, the little school project Shaylah was referring to involved the lives of hundreds of Elementals who all counted on her to protect them.

"Hey, did you see that video I sent you? It's hilarious!"

Ruby reached for her bag to grab her phone. She was glad Shaylah was switching topics. She rummaged through every pocket, finally dumping her bag upside down on the coffee table. "Crap!" she yelled as the contents of her bag spilled out.

"What's wrong?"

"I left my phone at the cente... At Liam's."

"It's fine, just look at the video tomorrow. I'm sure he'll love the excuse of having to see you again."

"No, it's not that. I had notes on there I needed," Ruby planned on going over the symbols again tonight, "I should probably go get it."

"Right now? Seriously?"

"It's fine. It's just a few subway stops. I'll be back

soon," she bolted up and ran to the door, "you going to bed soon?"

"Are you kidding? Hell's Kitchen is on reruns! I'll be up for hours!"

Ruby threw on her sneakers and ran down the stairs. A part of her was happy that she was mindless enough to forget her phone. Shaylah was right, she really needed to have some fun and the only person she wanted to have it with was still at the Elemental center.

CHAPTER 7
PAINTING THE STREET WITH
HER BLOOD

R uby was almost at the subway entrance when she heard footsteps behind her. The hair on her arms stood on its ends and an immediate sense of danger pulsed through her. She reached for her necklace, feeling its weight around her neck, making sure it was still in place. Her steps quickened and within seconds she was almost running to the subway. She could hear the footsteps behind her speed up to match her own.

The subway doors were so close that she could feel the rush of air from trains passing beneath her. Her strides grew longer and she was about to turn the corner when her hair pulled back. Her body yanked backward; she winced at the pain of thin strands of hair ripping away from her scalp. Ruby turned around to see the attacker but before she could make a full spin, an arm wrapped around her, dragging her back into an alley.

The darkness of the alley swallowed them as Ruby jabbed her elbow into her attacker's ribs. Remembering her training with Liam, she quickly jerked her other arm up behind her, making contact with what she was sure was a nose. She could feel warm liquid drip on her arm, with any luck, whoever was trying to hurt would now have some trouble breathing.

Ruby's body moved instinctively, pushing away and spinning to face the danger. She still couldn't see the person in front of her, it was as though they were pure darkness. A flashback to her vision introduced a new fear. Could this be what she was warned about?

The best move right now would have been to run. She knew if Liam was here, he'd push her back towards the street, to safety. But he wasn't here and she didn't care about being safe right now, she needed to see this bastard. As her assailant reached up to wipe their bleeding face, she planted one foot on the ground, spinning towards them and kicking them in the stomach. The attacker slid back, crouching over to ease the pain.

Her hands folded, beginning to shake from anger, a black fog pulsating between them. Ruby could feel her power tense within her, shaking her blood like a martini glass. She shoved her hands in her pockets before the fog crept out. She needed to be sure that she was fighting an Elemental before using her powers in the open. Seeing her hesitation, the attacker stood up taller, pushing off the ground in a run towards her. Ruby had no time to move out of the way, she charged forward, kicking her leg up mid-air. This time her kick managed to knock the stranger backwards, stumbling towards the only lit bulb in the alley. Revealing their face.

Ruby eyed the girl in front of her. She was young, about Ruby's age, maybe even younger. *Definitely younger.* Dressed in black from head to toe with the exception of a bright red scarf loosely tied around her neck. When she moved her head, her hair shone a deep purple hue making the sharp bangs look as though she was wearing a cap. If this wasn't how they first met, Ruby figured she might have even liked this girl. She moved her gaze up her attacker's body, meeting her eyes in a locked stare. Ruby gasped and jumped back. The stranger's eyes were pure black. Even the whites of her eyes were missing.

While she was examining the strangeness of her appearance, the assailant lunged forward, a cold grip locking around Ruby's necklace.

Oh, hell no! Ruby thought. *Human or not, this chick is not getting the sword piece.*

She moved her palms in front of the attacker's chest, closed her eyes and took a deep breath in. As she breathed out, she concentrated on her emotions, shifting them towards her hands. A surge of black smoke shot from her palms at the attacker, catapulting her against the wall behind them. Ruby could see her struggling to get up and turn to run. As the stranger ran into the darkness, she turned, flicking something in Ruby's direction.

The metal tip of the knife glistened as it passed through the light, back into darkness, hitting Ruby's arm at an impossible speed. Her entire body whipped around from the impact, pushing her to the ground. She looked down at her arm; in the dark she could see a stain starting to form on her t-shirt. Blood was soaking her favorite outfit.

Using her good arm to get herself up, she stumbled out of the alley and back to the street. She could feel herself grow weaker with each step but had to keep moving. Disoriented, she wobbled down the street towards her apartment. Painting the street with her blood as she walked.

CHAPTER 8
SOMETHING DARK

"Y ou're packing your things and coming to the center immediately." Liam was furious. She expected him to be, she did tell him that there was nowhere safer than her apartment, and then was beaten and stabbed in an alley the same day.

"You're overreacting. And you need to keep your voice down, Shay is right there." She gestured to the kitchen watching Shaylah load Jake up with a tray full of teacups. He almost tripped, catching his balance awkwardly, which made Shaylah laugh hysterically. A little too enthusiastically, in Ruby's opinion.

She sat up in her bed to get a better look at her wound. Liam did a pretty decent job wrapping it up, and to her surprise, once the bleeding stopped it turned out the cut was not as deep as she originally thought it was, "Is this looking like it's healing already to you or am I crazy?"

"It's definitely better now than it was an hour ago. Maybe it was just a scratch?" Liam noted but his face looked concerned.

"Ok, spit it out. What's that face for?" She asked, "you think it's weird, too, don't you?"

"I mean, it's definitely healing fast. Faster than I anticipated but again, the wound could have been just superficial."

"A superficial knife stab?" Ruby laughed. "Did it seem superficial when you pulled it out of my arm?"

"Wouldn't be the weirdest thing we've seen lately..."

"Holy crap, Fish!" Shaylah ran towards her, grabbing at her arm. "Are you, like, a superhero or something? This doesn't even look like it hurts anymore! When you rolled in here before, you looked like hell. I'm still not done bleaching your blood off the carpet."

"We were just saying that it probably looked worse than it actually is," Ruby said, giving a look to Liam that told him to keep quiet, "it honestly doesn't even hurt anymore. Maybe I'm just a bleeder or something."

Jake walked over, pushing his way past Liam with an arrogance she could do without. "Let me see that thing." He went to reach for her arm but she pulled back quickly.

"I'm fine, Jake."

"Yeah, Jake. She's fine." Shaylah teased. There was an odd tone in her voice and Ruby could have sworn it was a hint of jealousy.

"I don't need you guys swirling all over me. I was stupid to go off alone so late at night, but it was nothing more than a mugging gone wrong," her eyes met Liam's as she lifted the Onyx necklace off her chest, "I'm pretty sure whoever it was just wanted my necklace."

Liam's face tensed, his lips tightening into a straight line. He put both his palms on her cheeks, stroking them with his fingers. She could feel the heat of his emotions pushing into her skin, his fear was burning him up. "I don't know what I'd do if something happened to you."

"I'm going to go get a drink." Jake walked off, rolling his eyes, followed immediately by Shaylah.

"I know. I'm sorry I scared you. But it was just a close call, I have a feeling that we'll be having a lot of these soon."

"What do you mean?"

"I saw something today, when I hit that girl with my powers."

"Saw what exactly?"

"I don't even know how to describe it. Her eyes, they were pitch black."

"Lots of people have dark eyes, Rue."

"No, you don't get it. They were covered in something. Something dark. Evil almost."

"What do you think it was? Something Elemental?"

"I don't know," she squeezed his hand, "but whoever she was, she's connected to the Water piece theft. I just know it."

CHAPTER 9

ALL LEADERS HAVE SCARS

"How do you know she had something to do with it?" Liam's arm wrapped around her waist, pulling her close into safety.

"She wanted the necklace. She could have tried to steal anything else from me, I mean, my bag was literally just lying on the ground the whole time. But this was the only thing she was after." Her hand gripped the onyx stone tightly. She was never going to leave it unprotected, again.

"You think this has something to do with your vision?"

"I don't know. Maybe."

"Was there anything else about her that you remember? Any marks or something different?"

"Not really. Other than those eyes, she seemed

almost..." Ruby thought of a way to describe her, "Like me, actually."

"Like you how?"

"Just something about her seemed so familiar."

"Have you seen her before?" She could feel him tense up next to her, as much as she didn't like his over protectiveness, it was nice to have someone care about her this much. Ruby had gotten so used to having only a few people in her life that she still found it surprising how close she'd let him get to her. It was as though they'd known each other their entire lives. She glanced in Jake's direction, feeling a rush of guilt run through her. It wasn't that long ago that she had the same familiarity with him.

"I don't think so," she said bringing her attention back to Liam, "I would remember those eyes."

"We should probably talk to the elders about this."

"We will. But not right now. I don't want them taking their attention away from figuring out those symbols. The sooner we find out what they mean, the sooner we can find whoever took the sword. And if I'm right and this girl is involved, well, two birds with one stone."

"And how do we keep you safe in the meantime?"

"We don't."

"You know that's not an option, right?"

"Liam. We've already had this conversation. I

promise I will be more careful, but you can't watch me twenty-four seven."

"Actually, I can," he smiled, but she couldn't help but wonder if he was serious.

"Very funny. Look, I told you I'll come to the center, and I will. I just need a bit more time to make sure Shaylah doesn't get suspicious. You know how she gets when she thinks someone is keeping something from her."

Liam laughed, rubbing his hard shoulder against her cut and sending a painful chill down her arm. She pulled away quickly, cupping the wound as if to protect it. "I'm so sorry! Are you ok?"

"It's fine. I forgot it was there, too. I guess it's not as healed as I thought it was."

"Maybe we should take you to the hospital to get it checked out?"

She wiggled into him, placing her head on his shoulder. "I think I got pretty good medical attention already."

The joking tone in her voice seemed to have done the trick. Liam's shoulders relaxed and he quickly kicked off his boots to lounge in the bed next to her. "So, what's our next move?"

"Well, you had a good point before. With all of this worry about the symbols, I haven't had a chance to train at all. I have to get some more practice hours in, who knows what we should be expecting. I have to be ready to fight no matter what happens."

"You think something big is coming?"

"I'm not sure. But I don't want to be caught off guard if another Elemental war is brewing. We need to be prepared for whatever comes our way."

She squeezed in tighter to him. The wound on her arm still hurt but she pushed through the pain, letting his arms pull her tighter, enveloping her in a cocoon of his warmth. Her thoughts drifted off periodically only to be jolted back each time he took a breath and put pressure on the wound. The pain was a good reminder.

All leaders have scars, she thought before falling asleep on Liam's shoulder.

CHAPTER 10

WAR IS WAR

Ruby's face was bright red and her breathing shallow and fast. She twisted out of the way, barely avoiding the boulder Leah hurled towards her. Her vision was disoriented and without noticing, she bumped her right arm directly against the wall. The wound from the knife had healed already but a phantom pain made her cringe on impact.

"Omg! Are you ok?" Leah shouted, starting to run towards her.

"Better than you'll be soon," Ruby laughed.

She planted her feet on the floor and readied herself to run. Picking up speed and sprinting towards Leah, she let her hands meet as she ran, painting the air with fog. Encasing her in blackness. The fog spiralled around her, making her heart beat faster with each turn it made past her body. She focused her gaze on Leah, feeling her sudden panic. Ruby hurled herself upwards, trailing a mist of black fog behind her. Lunging at her opponent, she turned her thoughts inward, reaching deep inside herself, she let her emotions take over. Every fear, anger, happiness. Swirling and mixing within her. She flung her hands in front, directing a blast of energy at Leah's feet. Ruby had no intention of hurting her, this was just to teach her a lesson.

Before the fog reached its target, Leah shifted her balance, moving quicker than Ruby had expected her to. A wall of rock grew before Ruby's eyes, right in front of her jump path.

"Crap!" she yelled out and tried to get out of the way. Her hands shot up to break the impact causing her to lose her concentration. The black fog dissipated and with her shields gone, Ruby flew into the fall, bouncing back upon contact.

She sat up on the floor, looking down at the road rash on her palms from the rocks. If she was going to be ready for whatever came next, she had to get better than this.

"Ruby! Oh no! Your hands!" Leah's face was shocked, she didn't even realize that she'd hurt her until her head popped around the wall.

"I'm fine. Don't worry. That's the whole point of training. To get hurt so we can get better, right?"

"I guess. I really didn't mean to. I saw you jump and I just panicked."

"Seriously, Leah. I'm ok. It's just a few scratches. Nothing that won't heal." Judging by how fast the knife wound healed, the scratches would be an easy fix. Her palms had already started to form a new layer of skin. Whatever this new development was in her powers, she liked it.

"What exactly happened here?" Liam voice filled the training room, "Finally found your match, Rue?"

"No way! She was probably just going easy on me."

"I really wasn't. My head's not in the game. I have to get better."

"Don't be so hard on yourself. There's a lot going on right now," he crouched next to her on the floor and her breathing slowed as he put her rough palms to his lips and kiss each hand, "Wanna try again?" He jumped to his feet, extending his arm to help her up. "Or are you scared I'll hurt you?"

That's it! I'm going to tear this guy a new one! Ruby was on her feet in seconds, her hands already heating up, smoke coming off each finger. Out of the corner of her eye she could see Leah scurry out of the room, throwing one of her big smiles their way before she closed the door.

Ruby's hands were flames, boiling at the fingertips and ready to attack. She pushed them towards Liam, shooting two fireballs on either side of him.

"Oh, so we're playing with fire today, young lady?

You know that's my thing, right?" he chuckled, ducking quickly out of the way.

Her flames hit the wall behind him and extinguished like two birthday candles blown out. Disappointed, she readied for her next attack but before she could strike, a flame shot at her side, the impact twirling her across the room. She glanced at the sooty streak on her shoulder.

"Hey! This was my favorite t-shirt!" she yelled, and turned to face Liam.

"Are you going to fight me or worry about dry cleaning?"

"That's it! You're dead!" she shouted and darted towards him. She could see his hands ready for another shot. Her mind moved quickly, shifting through memories to find something sad to hold onto. The only thing that was clear was losing Jake's friendship. His lies, his father's betrayal, Liam's death. Tears welled up in her eyes and she used every piece of them. Her body was dripping wet with sweat and her face covered in saline. She moved the wetness towards her hands, directing them at Liam's fireballs and dousing him with a burst of water, extinguishing their danger immediately.

"Well played," he said. Before she could attack again, a line of fire formed from his feet to hers. She watched as Liam disappeared before her eyes, becoming one with the flame. She blinked her eyes trying to see through the smoke and flames. A second later, a finger tapped her on the shoulder. Looping around, she felt him behind her and knew it was too late. She'd lost the fight.

His crouched down, using his leg to trip her, knocking her down on the floor. Her back hit the cold cement, the wind knocked out of her like she had been keeping it prisoner for years and had finally opened the door. Ruby closed her eyes, her emotions swirling within her. She could hear Liam's voice in the background but pushed it away from her mind. She sank deeper into herself, latching onto the onyx around her neck, feeling it fill with her feelings. The room was spinning now. She didn't need to open her eyes to see it, knowing it was full of black fog. Ruby focused her breath, slowly bringing herself back to the room.

"Are you going to fight me or worry about dry cleaning?" Liam's familiar words rang in the room. Except this time, she didn't block the ball of fire hurtling towards her. She let it hit her, knock her down on the ground. She waited on the floor until she could hear Liam's footsteps rush towards her, right before he got near her, she filled her lungs with all the air she could breathe in. Her body floated off the ground, hanging above him, flying almost. When she was right on top of him, she forced the air out of her, falling on his body and pushing him down to the ground with her own weight.

She felt victorious, sitting on his chest and holding an imaginary blade to his neck. "Game over," she smiled and started to pull away. His arm held her in place, not letting her get up.

"Cheater," he grinned.

"What are you talking about?"

"I know you travelled back; I can feel it when you do."

She wondered if that was true. Could he really know when time had been altered? And if he could, was there a chance he knew that he had died the night of the peace treaty? She'd never told him about what had happened when she travelled back in time then. Just that it didn't work out like they had planned. Ruby couldn't bear to see him go through the trauma that news could bring. As strong as he was, she wanted to protect him from that ugliness.

"War is war. There is no cheating. Just winning."

She pushed her hands against his chest, using it to stand up again, but he wrapped his arms tightly around her before she even made it to her feet. Twisting his body on top of hers, he had her pinned in moments. Her body weak from his weight, she relaxed, letting him trap her in himself. Her legs wrapped around his waist, pulling him closer. She pushed her face to meet his, her mouth opening lightly as it met his bottom lip.

This was one fight she found worth losing.

CHAPTER 11
YOU COULDN'T HAVE KNOWN

Ruby's hands were still wrapped around Liam when the door creaked open. The two of them jumped back from each other, startled by the footsteps entering the room. As busy as the center was these days, it was hard for them to get time alone. There was always an interruption, and in this case, Ruby had a feeling that something urgent was headed their way. People usually tried to steer clear of their training sessions unless it was absolutely necessary.

"I thought I'd find you here!" Zag's shabby head emerged through the half open door, "Alice wants to see you."

"Right now?"

"Yeah, girl. She said it can't wait."

Ruby pushed herself back up, dusting off the dirt

from her pants and tucking her messy hair back into place. "Okay, we'll be right there."

"Oh, sorry. She said just you."

Her eyes drifted to meet Liam's. It's odd that Alice only wanted to see her, she trusted Liam with everything. This can't be good. She could see from Liam's furrowed brow that he felt the same confusion. What was going on?

They followed Zag away from the training rooms to Alice's quarters. Ruby had only been to visit Alice in her private room once and she remembered how uncomfortable she felt. She wasn't looking forward to spending more time there. She knocked lightly on the door, waiting for someone to answer then pushed her way in. Her eyes wandered to Liam as she closed the door behind her, wishing that he could follow her in.

The air in the room shifted when she finally turned around to face Alice. A gulp caught in her throat when she saw the other elders in the room; as far as she knew, this wasn't a scheduled elder meeting.

She scanned the vastness of the room, still not used to how different it looked from Liam's quarters and her own little cubby when she stayed here. The door of Alice's quarters opened to a large sitting area. There were two couches facing each other with a glass coffee table between them. Ruby's eyes twinkled from the light bouncing off the chandelier tears, its speedy dance covering the heads of the elders. They seemed on edge;

something had definitely happened while Ruby was in training. She tried to learn the secret they were guarding, but their faces were rigid, betraying no truth of the occurrence.

"Thanks for coming, Ruby." Elena said, "We know you probably have a lot going."

"It's no problem. Just wondering what's going on." She walked over to the coffee table and plopped down on the carpeted floor. "Did something happen?"

"To start, we just want you to know that we trust your opinion," Myriam's quiet voice barely reached her, "so whatever you think we should do in this situation is what we will go with."

"Okay..."

Alice walked over to her side, placing a light hand on her shoulder, hitting Ruby with a strong whiff of her perfume as she approached. The scent of cedar and musk lingered in the air when she spoke. "You're right to think something has happened."

"Alice, you don't have to sugar coat it. Just tell me what's going on."

"Another piece of the sword has been taken."

"What? Which one!?!" Ruby's eyes widened. She was shocked, after the first theft they put extra guards on the doors of the other safes. No one was supposed to be able to get in or out.

"The Earth piece is gone. Harvey went to check this morning and found the safe empty," Myriam squeezed

Harvey's hand in encouragement, "it's not your fault, Harv. You couldn't have known."

"I should have been checking on it more often after the Water piece went missing." His eyes met Ruby's but he quickly looked down at his hands.

"It's nobody's fault. I'll need to see the room, there might have been more symbols left that could help us figure out who's behind this."

"Did you see any symbols when you were in there?" Cyril's eyes made a beeline for Harvey, "Or anything out of the ordinary?"

The room went silent. The elders all watched Harvey intently, waiting for him to recall the scene. His brows furrowed, making the deep wrinkles on his forehead stand out even more. Ruby needed to get to the safe room as soon as possible. She looked up at Cyril, straightening herself to stand. "I don't think the symbols were meant for him."

"What do you mean?"

"I need to get to the safe room right away. Can we get Liam in here and brief him on what happened?" She was still upset that he couldn't be here in the first place, talking about it twice was just a waste of everyone's time.

"Of course. I thought it was best to tell you first so you could decide what you want to do." Alice said.

"I know, but from now on just assume that he should be here. He goes where I go."

CHAPTER 12

THE ALLEY GIRL'S EYES

R uby's mind was drawing a blank. She was right about there being symbols on the safe in Harvey's office, but there was nothing new about these marks. They were the same circles and crisscrossed lines she saw in the safe after the Water piece had been taken. She stayed in the office for hours, covering the room in black fog and pushing herself to the brink of exhaustion, until Liam dragged her away. Her body was weak from using her powers, overcome by all the emotions she had to tap into to fog the room.

As they got closer to his room, she could feel herself sinking. Her head was spinning, making her eyes water heavily. Ruby's arm reached for the wall to steady herself but she miscalculated how far away she was and ended up stumbling over instead. Liam caught her side quickly, scooping her up in his arms and carrying her towards the bed.

When her body hit the mattress, she finally let herself relax. Shutting her eyes slowly, she drifted into a deep sleep.

"I'll be right here when you wake up." She heard him whisper, but she was already too far gone to respond.

THE HAIR *on her arms was standing straight up from the chill. She felt disoriented, trying to push her eyes to the brim of focus. Her hands moved alongside her, trying to find the warmth of Liam's bed but all she could feel was roughness. Pushing herself up to sit, she looked down to find herself sitting on dirt-covered cement. She was no longer in Liam's room.*

Her eyes jumped from one wall to the next, trying to find a clue as to her location. There was a familiarity in this place, something rigid and eerie.

The Alley! She thought, and jumped to her feet, knowing full well who else was here with her last time.

She scanned the area, her gaze landing on a figure sitting under the only lit lamp, just a few feet away from her.

Slowly, she moved closer to the light, her eyes fixed on the figure and ready to attack at any moment. Her steps slowed and she could see the girl's chest moving up and down. She was definitely alive but why was she not moving?

Ruby crouched in front of her attacker. The top of the girl's hoodie covered her face and she could not get a clear look at her features. Not that she needed to see her to know who it was; the same necklace thief from before. Her hair poked out of the hoodie, layers of dark purple falling on a red scarf.

She knelt closer to her face, waving a hand in front of her. No reaction.

This was her chance to get some answers, to see who it was that attacked her. This could be the answer they'd been looking for this whole time, a lead to whoever stole the pieces of the sword.

Pushing through her fears, she moved her shaking hands towards her jacket hood. Lowering it slowly, hoping not to wake up her up from whatever trance she was in. The hood dropped to the girl's shoulders and Ruby fell back, staring at the face in stupor.

Disbelief crowded every inch of her body as she stared ahead. Her own face looking back at her as if she was facing a mirror.

SHE WOKE up abruptly in a sweaty mess. Her hair stuck to her forehead as she tried to breathe. She felt as though she had been underwater without an air tank and had finally made it to the surface.

Liam rushed to her side from his desk, holding her face in his hands and breathing almost as rapidly as she was. When she was finally able to meet his eyes, she saw fear in them. What was he seeing in her that made him so afraid?

"Liam? What's wrong? What happened?"

"Uhm..." he had no words.

"What is going on?!?" she pushed away from him, scrambling to her feet.

His hands moved down from her face to her shoulders, squeezing them in reassurance. She knew this move, he was trying to make sure she stayed calm, that she didn't overreact about whatever he was about to drop in her lap. Her mom used to pull this move on her when she was little. It never worked. "I don't want you to freak out," he said, "but you should probably go look in the mirror."

She pushed him out of the way, running towards the small bathroom in his room. The door banged against the wall when she slammed it open, bouncing back a little towards her. Her eyes locked on the small, oval mirror above the sink.

Ruby's hands squeezed the sides of the sink, she could feel her Earth powers kicking in but did not care to stop them. The marble creaked and crushed between her fingers as she looked at herself, studying the reflection in the mirror.

It was her all right. All one hundred and five pounds of her. Long messy hair forming sweaty shags around her shoulders. Her skin was as pale as always with just a slight hint of color in her cheeks. She was the same Ruby she had seen in the mirror a million times before. Except for the eyes staring back at her, piercing through to the core of her being. Jet black with not a hint of white. The alley girl's eyes.

CHAPTER 13
DRAWN TO HER

It was a few hours before Ruby's eyes regained their normal color. The darkness that lingered in them dissipated like a viral disease leaving her bloodstream. She ran to the bathroom every ten minutes, watching the veiny black lines get smaller and smaller until they were completely gone.

Liam reached for her eyelids, making her jerk her head back, she hated people touching her eyes. "Well, they look completely normal now."

"Great," she pulled her knees up to her chest. The entire experience made her feel almost violated somehow.

"What do you think that was exactly?"

"I have no idea. One minute I was asleep and the next..." she remembered the vision she had while sleeping, the girl in the alleyway and her own blank face.

"Did it hurt?"

She wanted to describe to him how it felt, what it was like to see herself through that darkness. But there were no words that would help him understand exactly what just happened. As much as she wanted him to feel like she trusted him, there was nothing about this that he could relate to. How could he? She could barely understand it herself. "No. Just weird to see that."

Something about the girl in the alley was important. She was drawn to her, like they were connected in some inexplicable way. She could feel it in her vision and then again later when looking at the darkness filling her eyes. But what did her vision mean? Why did she see herself transform into her own attacker? Ruby felt like she was missing an important part in the vision, some piece of the puzzle that could help her clarify everything that had been happening. She searched her memories of the vision for clues, when it suddenly hit her.

If she was somehow connected to the alley girl, did that mean Ruby had some link to the thefts? And if that was true, what was her involvement in all of it?

She needed to figure it out. There was still so much about her AetherBorn background that she didn't know. What if that was somehow related to all of this? So far, the symbols had been a dead end, but maybe they had been looking at this all wrong. Instead of trying to find clues in what was in front of them, they should have been looking for clues in what they knew nothing about. The AetherBorns.

"Hello? Earth to Rue? You still with me?" Liam waved his hand in front of her face trying to get her attention.

"Oh. Sorry. I just blanked there for a second."

"Did you hear anything I said?"

She hadn't. Whatever his plan was, she knew he had to work on it alone, she was already one step ahead of him. "Sorry."

"It's ok. I was just saying that we should tell Alice about your eyes, maybe she'll know something."

"Yeah, sure. You should tell her."

"You don't want to come with me?" She could see the disappointment in his eyes, he was used to them doing everything together. But this was different, it's not that she didn't trust him to help her, just that she knew she could speed up the process if they split up. And right now, there was no time to be wasted.

"I was thinking I might go put in some more work on the symbols. I kinda need a break from elder business for a bit, if you know what I mean."

"Yeah, I guess," Liam reached over and kissed her cheek then got up to leave, "meet later for dinner?"

"For sure! You know I'll never say no to food!" she said.

As she watched him walk away, sadness rushed through her. She had not kept anything from him since they started seriously seeing each other. She felt like she was betraying their entire relationship by keeping him out.

Shaking the thoughts off, she sprinted from the bed, ready to hit the books in the library. If she was right and she had a connection to the thefts she needed to find out what that connection was. It was starting to look like she might be the only one who could stop whoever was stealing the sword pieces. Or at least, the only one who had the most to lose. The symbols, her attack in the alley, Ruby was being targeted. She needed to know why, and by whom.

Tucking one of the notebooks from Liam's desk under her arm, she let the door slam shut on her way out. Locking her out of the safety of his room and pushing her towards answers she wasn't sure she wanted to find.

CHAPTER 14

CLUES IN HER RAMBLINGS

The books around Ruby looked like a fortress of knowledge. She had been researching for hours and was getting tired of hitting dead ends. Every piece of information about the AetherBorns that she was able to uncover only led to more questions. It was as though someone had completely wiped their history from existence.

She rested her face in her hands, defeated. The library in the training center had the most extensive collection of books on Elementals Westerlake had to offer. After the treaty, the elders collected every text each house had and brought them all here in hopes of creating a knowledge base they could use to train new Elementals. But so far, all of the information pertained only to Elemental powers and some history on each of the houses. There was barely any mention of Aether-Borns in sight.

The only thing Ruby was able to uncover thus far was that the first AetherBorn was part Elemental and part deity, having been created with the help of Aether, one of the original primordial Gods. These were all things she already knew, not at all helpful in her search for answers. Ruby ran her fingers down a page, scanning the words quickly. She was about to close the book she held and move to the next, when her eye caught the mention of a name. Eirene.

There was something different about this name from the rest of the names thrown her way in the last few hours. It somehow felt familiar. Her eyes widened as she read the passage.

'From fear of losing the only thing she loved more than him, Eirene hid the child from the elders, leaving her with a family she knew she could trust. The girl was never to be seen again.'

This was it! Eirene must have been the first Aether-Born! Ruby almost jumped for joy. She finally had a starting point.

Having a name gave her an in to finding out more. But where to go next? This was the only mention of her in the Elemental library and she doubted she could find anything else on the subject.

Ruby had a million questions. What happened to Eirene's daughter? What family did she leave her with?

And who was the man the passage referred to? He was clearly very important to Eirene but there was nothing else about him written here.

She jotted down her notes in the notebook, reading over them again and again, hoping to spark an idea. It felt like she was on the brink of answers but something just didn't sit well with her. Harvey and Myriam had been going over the texts for weeks, looking for anything on the symbols, with no results. And now she finally found a hint at AetherBorn history but it was also a dead end.

Maybe we're looking in the wrong place. She thought. *Wait...*

She pushed a few books off the top of one of the stacks, picking up a massive text that resembled an old encyclopedia. Her fingers ran along the spine, feeling each raised letter of the title. The Symbology of Elementals.

This was the book they'd been using to try and make sense of the symbols left in the safes after the sword thefts. All of the symbols here were those of Elemental houses. They had been trying to see if the symbols were a combination of some of the house symbols. But what if the symbols they saw had nothing to do with Elementals? What if they were AetherBorn symbols?

It would make sense they wouldn't find information on them here. AetherBorns were not a part of modern Elemental culture.

Ruby pushed the book out of the way and grabbed her notebook. She knew exactly where to look next. She ran back to Liam's room, determined to get to the bottom of things. Rushing to get her phone from her bag, she dialed a number, her hands shaking with excitement. "Hi, mom?" She said breathlessly, "Do you still have grandma's journals? From when she was in the institution?"

"Oh. I think your dad has them tucked away somewhere. Why? What's wrong?"

Ruby's heart beat faster. The only other symbols she had seen, other than these books, were in her grandmother's files in Dr. Olivian's office. She knew her grandmother kept a journal when she was institutionalized, but it never occurred to her to check there. This entire time, she'd been looking for clues in Elemental history, thinking their books would have the most concise information. What she should have been doing was getting information from another AetherBorn. Just because everyone thought she was crazy didn't mean her grandmother did not leave important knowledge behind. There could be crucial clues in her ramblings. "Nothing's wrong. I'll be there soon. Ask dad to find the journals please.

"And mom?" she paused, "I'm going to need to see the family albums."

CHAPTER 15

CLEAR AS DAY

"Honey! You want some more tea?" her mom yelled from the kitchen.

They had been going over her grandmother's journals for about an hour now and most of the notes they found so far had been nonsensical. Pages upon pages of gibberish from someone who was definitely not in their right mind. Reading through them made Ruby feel nauseous with sadness, that is when she wasn't pissed off. Her grandmother was just like her, pushed into a world of demi-Gods and AetherBorns, but she didn't have the support system Ruby had. She didn't have Liam or her parents. She got dragged from her family and pushed into an institution, labelled with some disease and left to rot. Ruby couldn't help but think that she could have ended up in the same situation if she didn't have anyone who believed in her.

"Sure, why not. Thanks!" She turned the page of yet another journal, searching through pages of scribbles and symbols. Her eyes scanning each word twice, hoping to have it lead somewhere. "Any luck, dad?"

"I got nothing so far," her father sat across her in his reading chair, his eyes moving as fast as Ruby's through his own pile of notebooks, "the same symbols over and over."

She thought about how hard this must be for him. He had been so young when his mother killed herself, and she was sure he still didn't quite understand it. Being a man born into an AetherBorn line meant he had none of the abilities Ruby and her grandmother possessed. The only understanding he had of their powers was from the bits and pieces he found in her journals. And whatever he remembered from the stories she shared with him before she died, hanging herself in her room with rope she'd stolen from the janitor's room. He was the one who found her there, he and his father, on one of their weekly visits. Ruby's mother told her that they wouldn't take her down until the police cleared the scene, they just left her hanging for hours. The thought of it made Ruby sick, what people could do to one another. It was no wonder her dad barely spoke of her. She was pretty sure that until Ruby gained her own powers, he was likely hoping the AetherBorn story was just a fairytale his mother made up before giving up on life entirely.

"Wait," he straightened his reading glasses and squinted his eyes to read, "this one line here, I can't quite make it out."

Ruby ran to his side, hoping she can get a clearer look. "I can see... wait, what's that word there? It's so scribbled."

"Layla! Darling, can you come here? You might be able to make it out," her dad gave Ruby a wink, "your mom has eagle eyes, you know." He said in a whisper.

"Which word? And don't think I can't hear your little jokes," her mom smiled, giving her dad a small smack in the back of the head. "This one here?"

"Yes, can you make it out?"

"Them. I think it says: I can see them now. Clear as day. With their black..." she pushed her layered bangs out of her eyes and leaned in, "I can't figure out the last word. It's scratched out."

"Eyes," Ruby said, not needing to look to know what the word was, "their black eyes."

"Well, that's odd. What do you think it means?"

She looked at her parents, not wanting to drag them into this mess but knowing full well that she needed all the help she could get if she was to stop the danger looming over the Elementals.

"It means we're in trouble," she said with a heavy sigh.

CHAPTER 16
THEY'RE GOING TO LOVE YOU!

"So, you think your grandma knew something about the symbols?" Liam asked, gesturing to the journals she brought back to the center. She had packed up everything she could find of hers at her parents' house, and took a cab back that evening. The journals were the only thing they had leading them to information on the AetherBorns, and she couldn't risk them getting into the wrong hands. The center was the only place she could think of that was guarded enough to store them.

"I'm not sure. But it's obvious that the girl in the alley was not the only one. My grandmother saw more people like her."

"Or she saw a vision and was too drugged up to know what it meant."

"Could be," she hadn't considered that option yet, "she *was* in a mental institution after all. I guess it's possible it was just a vision of what happened to me?"

They sat in silence, leafing through the journals. Usually, Ruby was grateful for being able to spend time with Liam without having to speak. It was as if they understood each other beyond the use of words. But right now, she wished for nothing else than to hear what he was thinking, to see if his assumptions aligned with hers.

"Wait, what words did she use exactly?" Liam asked, reading her to a tee.

"I can see them now. Clear as day. With their black eyes," she answered, "then it's just a bunch of random drawings of eyes."

"So, it wasn't a vision. At least not of you and the girl in the alley."

"How do you figure?"

"Well, she said 'they.' That girl is the only one you've seen with black eyes. Except..." he paused and looked at her.

"Except for me the other day?"

"Yeah," he raised one eyebrow, "either way, your grandmother wrote that she saw several people with black eyes."

"So?"

"So, there must be more of them. Whoever they are."

Ruby ran towards him, jumping on his lap and wrapping her arms around him as tightly as she could get them. His neck smelled of cologne, a mix of spicy musk and African violet. She pressed her lips against his, taking in the hot air he breathed out. "You're brilliant!"

"Huh? I mean, I obviously am but why this time?" he shifted his weight, causing her to fall over onto the bed, her legs still resting on his muscular thighs.

"The girl in the alley, she's the answer! If there are more like her, then finding her is the key to all of this."

"What about these journals? There's still so much here to go through, what if there are more hints that your grandmother left that could help us?"

"Ok. How about you stay and go over these, and I'll see if I can find this girl, then?"

"Yeah, that's not going to happen," he said, clearly upset with her suggestion, "you're definitely not going on your own after the creep that stabbed you."

"So, what's your plan then? You want us to sit around reading while she goes through with whatever scheme she has for the sword? What if grandma was right and there are more of them? What then?"

Her hands shook. She couldn't believe he would rather read through notes than look for the person who might be directly responsible for stealing the sword pieces. The Liam she chose to be with would never sit back from a fight, he was the first one to rush into it, no questions asked. What was going on here? Was everyone just going to sit by and wait until another war started?

"Rue, calm down," he reached for her hands, slowly extinguishing the fire forming in them, "I'm going to go with you to find her. Obviously. I'm just saying that these journals are the first pieces of information you have on where you come from. Don't you want to know if there is something here that could help us? Could help you?"

She immediately felt foolish. He wasn't backing down from a fight; he was just doing what he thought was best for her. Trying to help her understand where she came from. And he was right, she really did need to calm down. "So, what do you think we should do?"

"Well, I think you're right. We should definitely try to find this girl. Do you think Jake's dad would help?"

"Cyril? Why?"

"Look, I get you still haven't forgiven him for his part in the Elemental war, I haven't either. But you have to admit, he has a reach in this city that none of us have. He could pull some strings, throw his money around. Get some answers."

"It's not the war that made me hate him..." she said.

"Then what?"

"Nothing. It's not important. He's just not the best, ok?" she looked down at her hands, "but you're right, he can probably help."

"Great. So, we can go talk to him tomorrow."

"No. Let's ask Jake first. I want to involve him in this," She could see Liam's brow furrow at the mention of his name, "he said he wanted to be more involved, so let's involve him. It's only fair, he *is* the next in line for the elder spot in the Water house."

"Yes, of course, the prodigal Water prince. How could we forget." Liam rolled his eyes and looked away.

"Liam! Stop, please! He was my best friend long before all of this. I can't discount that; I think I made that pretty clear."

"Fine. But he doesn't get to lead this. You and I make all the decisions when we find this girl. Deal?"

"Yes, deal. Geez."

Ruby couldn't help but smile at his jealousy. He knew exactly how she felt about him so there was no need for him to act this way, but his reactions to Jake's presence made her understand just how much he cared about her. She should have been mad that he was acting like a child about it, but instead, she only wanted him more. "What about the journals?" she asked, switching the subject before the flush in her face gave her away.

"I was thinking we could recruit some help on these. The elders should take turns reading them, maybe there's something they can see in here that we can't. Also, Leah. She's kind of a whiz at research."

"Must be all those crime TV shows she watches," Ruby laughed. Leah was obsessed with television and almost every topic of conversation with her somehow led back to a show.

"And, Rue?"

"Yeah?"

"What about your dad? Do you think he might want to help?"

"Absolutely not," she pushed back from him and sat up on the bed, "I am not dragging him into this."

"But he knew your grandmother better than anyone. He might be able to make sense of some of this." His hands opened up one of the journals to a page full of messy-looking drawings.

"He was a kid when she killed herself. Whatever he might remember will probably not even be useful. It's bad enough he has to deal with his daughter being an AetherBorn, I'm not making him rehash his shitty childhood for no reason."

"But what if..."

"End of discussion, Liam. He is not to be involved unless there is no other way around it."

"Fine."

He started to get up but she pulled on the back of his shirt, forcing him to lie down next to her. She turned to her side to face him and placed her palm on his cheek. She could feel the stumble of his beard roughen up her fingers as she playfully danced her fingers across his skin. "If we absolutely need him, I will bring him in. I promise."

"Okay. Thank you."

"Hey! What about your parents?"

"What about them?"

"Think they might know something that can help? About the AetherBorn I mean?"

"About that," he paused, "I kind of had some news."

"News?"

"Well, you know how I said they moved to Italy a few years back?"

She did remember this, quite vividly. The idea of not having to meet Liam's parents until they had some more time to figure out their relationship was a massive relief. She wanted some time to find their own pace before going through the anxiety of meeting the parents. Liam had only met *her* parents a handful of times and they lived in the same city. And now with everything that was happening, meeting his parents was the last thing she wanted to add to her plate.

"Well, they're kind of coming back next week."

"What? I thought you said they didn't care for the Elemental world?"

"They didn't."

"So, what changed?" She asked then quickly realized she already knew the answer, "Oh. I get it."

"Rue, it's not you."

"Of course, it is! They heard you're dating an AetherBorn and are rushing back to save you from her. Great."

"That's not it. You know that."

"So, why are they coming back now of all times?"

"They're coming back to meet the sword keeper."

"So, me?"

"Yes, Rue, you. There hasn't been an AetherBorn in a very long time. My parents are pretty traditional when it comes to Elemental history. A new leader is a big deal to them. They never wanted to be around before because everything the resistance was doing went against tradition. The way they see it, your presence here means things are getting back to how they should be."

"So, they're traditional enough to want me around, but not so traditional that they believe that I should be some celibate little angel that's not allowed to date?" She thought back to everything she'd read so far about Eirene, the first AetherBorn. Her odds in the dating world weren't exactly stacking up high.

"They're not lunatics, Rue. They get that people date now."

"Just checking," she smirked. "I take it you didn't tell them about the missing sword pieces?"

"Not yet. Kind of putting that off for now."

"Awesome," she sighed, "and you're sure they're not here to get me out of your life?"

"Are you kidding? They're going to love you!" Liam exclaimed. His smile usually put her at ease, making her feel that everything would be just fine, but somehow this time she could find no solace in it. She wasn't just a leader anymore. She was a leader about to meet her boyfriend's parents for the first time. Because, that's what she needed right now, more pressure.

CHAPTER 17
FEVERISH FLAMES

R uby was walking in circles around the dining table. She could barely sleep last night, the news Liam dropped in her lap about his parents had her more on edge than she'd anticipated. With two sword pieces missing, and still not being any closer to finding the girl in the alley, she had more pressing matters to think about. But she couldn't help run every possible scenario of meeting his parents. She was never great at first impressions and this one had to be perfect. Ruby didn't just need to convince them that she was good enough for their son, she had to show them that she was a good enough leader for the Elementals. Liam's parents were very respected members of the house of Fire. Though not elders like Alice, they had proven themselves to be almost royalty amongst their people. When the resistance formed, they chose to stay out of the fight in order to uphold Elemental traditions set by ancient beliefs. Because of that strong sense of heritage, even the elders themselves carried a large amount of respect for the Nars. She often wondered why they weren't chosen as elders themselves instead of Alice. Although right now, she was more than grateful for that fact. Her skills as a leader were being tested daily and she would have hated to fail in front of them.

"Another turn and you'll rip a hole through the floor," Liam joked. He was reclining on one of the chairs, pushing it back to balance on two feet, looking as relaxed as ever.

"Huh?"

"You're pacing. You training for a marathon or something?"

She took a deep breath in and stopped in her tracks. How could he be so calm right now? There was so much they still needed to sort out. "Just freaking out a little, I guess. When's Jake getting here?"

"He said he'll be here soon, hopefully with some news."

"I don't know. If it was good news, he would've told us already." Her head dropped to the side, eyeing Liam's expression. She wondered if he could feel her anxiety right now. He was always so good at knowing what she was thinking, so much so that she barely ever had to tell him how she felt, but somehow right now it was as if they were not in tune. He had no idea how scared she was, if he did, he wouldn't be so calm.

"Speak of the Devil!" he yelled out and straightened his chair, "Rue is about to have an aneurism."

"Sorry, I got held up at the office," Jake said and made his way to the center of the cafeteria.

His suit was perfectly smooth as usual, leading her to believe he had just spent all morning in meetings with his father at the bank. Ever since the treaty, it seemed all of his free time was spent there. She knew he was being groomed to take over the elder seat but his absence from the center was deliberate. Like he was purposefully trying to avoid her and when he did speak to her, it was irritated and sarcastic. Ruby feared the day that he finally took on the role of elder, his hatred for Liam would be problematic at best. "So, what's the news? You said you had something."

"Straight to business, I see," He smiled, "How's it going, Jake? How was your morning? Watch any good shows lately?"

"Jake, come on!" She threw her hands up dramatically, "We don't have time for this! What did your dad's guy find?"

"Well..." he looked down.

"Nothing. He found nothing, right?"

"Not nothing. He almost had her."

"So, what happened?" Liam asked, walking over to Ruby. "Is there anything we can use?"

"This girl is good. I mean really good. My dad's security is the best in the business. If someone is alive, he can track them. But she was almost impossible to find."

"So, it's a dead end?" Ruby felt defeated. How would they ever get to the bottom of the sword thefts if they couldn't even find one girl in Westerlake.

"Not exactly. He was able to track her to Lakeside."

"On the other side of the city?"

"Yep. He followed her to some bar but when he went in, she was gone. Like vanished, gone."

"People don't vanish, Jake."

"Rue, come on. There're lots of things that *people* we know do..."

He had a point. Whoever this girl was, she wasn't human. But if she could just disappear on command, how were they supposed to find her? It took Ruby all of her powers to find the sword last time and that was a stationary object. How was she expected to get hold of a girl who could possibly vanish?

She could feel herself heat up. Her anger boiling every liquid within her. There was too much pressure on her. She knew when she took on the role of leading the Elementals it would not be an easy task but this was too much. She hadn't even had a chance to get used to it and there was already a disaster brewing. Ruby felt cheated, like she had been lied to once again. Her face was overheating, beads of sweat fell from her hair, down her neck and shoulders, sending puffs of steam as they hit her scorching body. Her head was spinning. She tried to focus her eyes but something was in the way. Flames. Feverish flames danced around her.

"Rue! Rue, calm down!" Liam's voice echoed somewhere behind her.

She tried to follow his direction, taking deep breaths in and slowly blowing them out. Holding onto the release, making it last longer, a trick she'd learned in hours of meditation when she first started training. But nothing worked. The fire rose around her, forming a heated wall of anger and hurt. If she didn't get her act together, she was going to burn down the entire cafeteria.

Panic rose within her. She had gotten good at harnessing her powers, why was she unable to stop right now?

Her mind was still racing when she felt a hand reach in to grab her arm. Liam's hand, wrapping around her, absorbing some of the flames. She heard him mumble something but couldn't make out the words. Within seconds, steam rose off her body and she was covered in snow. Her eyes opened to Jake's outstretched palms; tiny icicles covered his fingers. Liam pulled her into him. Rubbing his hand across the back of her head, trying to calm her down.

"What happened?" she asked, still disoriented from the heat.

"I have no idea. But if it wasn't for Jake extinguishing you with that blizzard, I don't know what would have happened," he nodded a quick thanks in Jake's direction. "Why didn't you stop?"

"I don't know. I tried to but I just couldn't."

"We need to get this checked out. If your powers are acting up, we need to fix it right away. It's fine down here, but what if this happened outside?"

She looked up at him, realizing quickly what he meant. If she couldn't control her own powers, she could seriously hurt people. Kill them even. She needed to figure out why she couldn't tap into her emotions. Something was blocking her, but what?

Great, she thought. *One more thing to add to the crap pile.*

CHAPTER 18
YOUR BEST FRIEND

"Can I talk to you?" Jake asked.

She had changed out of the snow-covered clothes and was back in the cafeteria, hoping to get some more information about the alley girl. Relieved she had kept a spare outfit in Liam's room, her mind was back in focus. She'd have to figure out her powers later, this was a priority.

"Sure, what's up?"

"Alone," Jake's eyes landed on Liam, asking him to leave.

She felt odd about Liam not being in the room with them. They hadn't spent any time alone since the night of the treaty, but if this was going to help her get her friend back then Liam would need to understand. She could see him watching her, waiting for what she said next. "Sure, you want to go to the library?" His smile dropped at her words, a flash of betrayal sprinting across his face.

"Well, this is awkward. I'll just leave, I have to go see Zag anyway." Liam got up and walked towards the door, giving her a kiss on the cheek on his way. She'd have to find a way to make it up to him later. When he was out of the room, she walked over to the table Jake was sitting at and perched on the edge.

"So, what's up?" she asked, truly not knowing what he was thinking.

"Look, Rue. I know things have been weird lately."

"I mean, things have not been the best, yes. But you've been especially weird. I just don't get it."

"You really don't get it?" he asked, "I don't think it's that hard to get, Rue."

"Why don't you explain it to me? Because it seems to me like you're pissed and you're taking it out on Liam."

"Jesus, Rue. Not everything is about Liam. I'm so sick of hearing his name all the time. You know, before *him* you were an actual person, right?"

"Hey! That's not fair! I have a lot going on now. I don't need you judging me on top of it all."

"I'm not judging you. I'm..." he paused.

"You're what?"

"I'm in love with you, Rue. Don't you get that? I can't just sit around and be okay with you two. I will never be okay with it!" Jake's voice got louder, "How can you choose him over me? After everything we've been through together?"

She moved closer to him, picking up his hand in hers. She could sense how hurt he was and hated that she was responsible for it. But there was nothing she could do to make it better. He would never let this go unless she made it completely clear, even if it meant hurting him even more. "Jake, I'm sorry. I never meant for any of this to happen. You know that." She squeezed his large palm in her hands, "Until I met Liam, you were my whole world."

"And now what? I'm nothing?"

"No. Not at all. It's just not the same. I wish it was different, I really do. But I can't help how I feel."

"You're honestly telling me that you're choosing that outsider over your best friend?"

"He's not an outsider, Jake. There are no sides anymore. I thought we'd made that pretty clear with the treaty."

"This isn't about the Elementals, Rue. What about how you feel?" he sighed, not wanting to hear her.

"That's what I'm trying to tell you. I love you, Jake, I really do. Just not like that," She leaned in closer to him, "I really want my best friend back. Can we try that at least?"

His hand jerked away from hers, his body drooping into a slump. She could see tears start to form in his eyes but he straightened up quickly, not letting his emotions betray him. He was his father's son after all. "I guess." He said and walked towards the door.

"Jake?" She shouted, watching him stop in his tracks, his back turned towards her. "I really do miss you; you know."

"Me, too," he whispered, and walked out of the room, leaving her completely alone.

CHAPTER 19
LAKESIDE

Lakeside looked particularly beautiful today. When they got off the streetcar at the last stop before the pier, Ruby could sense a shift in the atmosphere. They were only about an hour out of the city but the air smelled cleaner. Free of pollution somehow. And Elementals.

She was very aware of the fact that they were here on a mission, but something about being away from the center and the craziness of their lives there made it feel like a vacation.

They walked down the main street, looking around the windows of the small shops. Ruby's eye caught a trinket in one of the windows and ran over to take a closer look. Her eyes caught her own reflection in the window. She didn't feel much different, but the girl looking back at her was someone she didn't even recognize. She was taller somehow, more determined. Someone with the burden of the world weighing her down.

"You okay?" Liam's voice made her lose her thoughts. She watched him in the window in awe. How could somehow so perfect want to be with her? His arms wrapped around her, pulling her back into his chest. Leaning her head on his shoulder she let herself breathe freely for the first time since her talk with Jake. The hurt in his voice still hanging in her thoughts. Hurt she created.

"Yeah, I'm good. Just nice to get away, I guess."

"It really is beautiful here, isn't it?" He pulled her away from the window and they walked farther down the street, "we should come back for the weekend when..."

"When we're a normal couple?" she laughed.

"I was going to say when the weather isn't so hot, but yeah, when we're a normal couple."

"You think that's ever going to happen?"

He stopped, pulling her towards him and running his fingers through her hair. His lips reached over and grazed hers lightly, making her legs tingle with excitement. "We don't need normal, Rue. We're perfect just the way we are."

In the middle of a heat drenched street, she let him hold her like they were the only two people in the world. Memorizing every inch of his shoulders and back with her fingertips. They weren't perfect, she knew that for sure. But they were as close to happy as she could ever ask for. Standing here in the middle of the street with the warm wind from the pier hitting her back, she felt complete somehow. Like she was exactly where she needed to be.

"Come on," She said, tugging at his sleeve, "Let's go find this bar."

CHAPTER 20
RAY OF FREAKING SUNSHINE

The bar smelled of an unpleasant combination of grease and chlorine. Ruby couldn't imagine someone wanting to spend a long time in here, but it was still pretty full despite it being only four in the afternoon.

They looked around the tables, hoping to get lucky and spot the girl from the alley sitting down at one of them. When they didn't see anyone that matched her description, Liam suggested they grab a seat at the bar.

"Maybe she'll come in soon," he said, but Ruby could tell it was just an excuse for him to get her to relax.

They pulled up two rusty chairs and sat off to the side, careful not to attract attention to themselves. This was a pretty small neighborhood and they were certain that two strangers coming in from the city stood out like sore thumbs. Especially when those strangers kept staring at the door every time someone walked in.

"What can I get you?" the bartender asked, after ignoring them for a few minutes.

He was shorter than Ruby realized, and she had to push forward in her chair to see him more clearly. She couldn't quite pinpoint his age. His ripped jeans and band tee made him look like he was younger than his receding hairline implied. She was still eyeballing him when Liam nudged her side to snap out of it. "Oh. I'll have a coffee if you have one."

"We don't do coffee here. You want a beer?"

"Uhm, no it's okay," she wanted to keep a clear head in case the girl showed up, "just a water is fine."

"I'll have a beer!" Liam exclaimed, "What's on tap?"

"We're just switching the taps. I have a few bottles of Lakeside Pine if you want that in the meantime?"

"Sure, why not."

The bartender popped open a bottle cap and slammed the beer in front of Liam causing a bit of froth to pour out. "So, what brings you guys to Lakeside?"

"I guess it's pretty obvious we're not from here?" Liam continued making small talk.

"Not really. But we're kind of a regular spot for this place. Never seen you two before, that's all."

"We're looking for someone," Ruby jumped in, "a girl."

"There's lots of girls that come here, miss. You'll have to be more specific."

The word miss hung in the air like a cat hiss in a hollow room. Ruby wasn't sure when she became a 'miss' but she didn't have a taste for it. "She's about my height. Skinny. Probably lots of black clothes. Her hair is like this really dark shade of purple and last time I saw her she had a red scarf on, like a bandana or something."

"She missing or something?"

"No, nothing like that." Ruby tried to think of a convincing lie, "She's supposed to sell me her camera. We met her in one of the shops down the street earlier but I'm an idiot and forgot to get her number. She mentioned coming here before, so I figured might as well give it a shot." She reached into her bag, pulled out her own camera and put it on the bar. "I could really use an upgrade." Liam pinched her leg, a smile on his face. Clearly, he was impressed with her lying skills.

"You said she had a red bandana on?" the bartender asked.

"Yeah. Bright red. You know her?"

"Sounds like it could be Ray. She's here a lot. Usually comes in around this time."

"Ray? Odd name choice." Liam noted.

"Not if you get to know her."

"Why's that?"

"Cause she's a ray of freaking sunshine," the bartender laughed and walked away.

Ruby's mouth leapt into a smile. They were in the right place! All they had to do was stick around for a bit and hope this Ray made it in today. But what if she knew they were looking for her? Jake said that his dad's security followed her here and she disappeared. Why disappear if you don't think you're being followed? She was about to ask Liam what he thought when the bell on the front door jingled. She turned quickly to see who was coming in and froze.

"Looks like you're getting that camera after all!" The bartender yelled out, "Yo! Ray! These guys have been looking all over town for you!"

The girl's eyes darted to Ruby and her mouth gaped open. She wasn't expecting them to find her so quickly it seemed. Ruby got off her chair, starting to walk towards her but before she could get even halfway there, the bell on the door rang furiously.

Ray was on the run.

CHAPTER 21
I PROMISE

Ruby's steps widened until she was almost leaping from foot to foot down the street. As soon as she realized that Ray ran off, she took after her without so much as a second thought. She hoped that Liam was right behind her, but couldn't check. This was their chance to get this girl and she wasn't about to take her eyes off her for a second.

She watched Ray's purple locks bounce as she ran, dodging passerby's like an Olympic medalist. Her short legs moving faster with each sprint. Before Ruby could react, she saw her turn the corner into a small cafe. She ran faster, hoping Liam saw her go inside.

The cafe was narrow and long with a coffee bar along the right wall and minimal seating on the left. The entire middle section of the room was filled with people waiting to place their order. Ruby's eyes searched the area, quickly noticing a red dot disappear towards the back. Ray's scarf gave her away in the crowd like a beacon. She pushed people out of the way, making her way to the back.

"Sorry! Excuse me!" she heard Liam's voice behind her, relieved he was still there.

There was a set of doors at the end of the hallway, barely visible from the front but a definite exit. Ray knew this town well it seemed; they were at a disadvantage but Ruby refused to give up. She bolted through the doors, her breath shallow and quick. She was trying to decide whether to turn left or right when the doors opened behind her.

"Which way, Rue?" Liam asked.

"Not sure. You go left and I go right?"

"Sure. Don't do anything stupid!" he yelled as he disappeared.

Ruby ran in the opposite direction of him, finding herself in a tapered alley. It felt colder than the rest of the town. And darker somehow. *What is with this chick and alleys,* she thought and crept forward.

Her steps slowed down as she made her way down the alley. Something didn't feel right. She was being watched; she could feel eyes on her but couldn't see anyone around. She searched the area, noticing the rows of garbage bags that adorned the back of the doors, this must be the other side of the street they were on before. The dirty side no one gets to see.

She kicked a fast food bag out of the way, tossing it towards one of the dumpsters. Her breath stopped, there was a hint of red shining from between two large bins. She almost missed it walking by, but was sure now. In the darkness, Ray was hiding, waiting to make her move.

Moving the palms of her hands closer together, she crouched into a defensive stance. Her feet planted solidly on ground, looking at the red dot. "I know you're in there!" she yelled, a ball of fire forming in her hands.

The darkness moved slightly like a wind blew through it. She concentrated, watching as Ray slowly stepped into the alley, her black eyes trained on Ruby's hands.

"I don't want to hurt you. I just want to ask a few questions," she said, lowering the fireball as a peace offering, "I promise." She was about to extinguish it completely when the sound of footsteps approached them.

There was no time to let Ray know that it was safe, that the Elemental next to them was just Liam. A friend. She watched Ray's hands go up defensively, black fog pushing away from them, surrounding every inch around her and Liam.

She could hear him coughing, waving his arms around the fog and trying to disperse it. She knew it wouldn't work. This wasn't some parlor trick, it was the same fog Ruby could conjure when she focused her emotions. She stepped forward, moving through the fog with ease, it didn't have the same hold on her as it did on Liam. Ray had already taken this chance to run off down the alley, another minute and she'd be lost to them. She couldn't let that happen.

Her hands were stretched to the sides as she walked towards Ray, ripping through the brick on the buildings on either side until they buckled out of the walls one by one. She pointed her hands at the ground behind Ray, connecting to its element. As she lifted her arms up, a wall of earth and cement rose, trapping Ray in a dead end. She could see her panic, look for a way out then start to mumble something. As she spoke, black fog gathered around her, circling faster and faster, threatening to take her away.

Ruby ran towards the darkness. "You're not getting away that easily!" she yelled. She trained her hands at Ray's chest and pictured the air in her lungs. Holding onto the image, Ruby pushed deep inside of herself, manifesting every bit of happiness to connect to her Air powers. As she raised her fists, she could see the fog drop away from Ray, her hands raising to her neck, struggling to breathe.

"Ruby! Stop! We need her alive!" Liam yelled, pushing past her towards Ray.

She watched as he picked her up, shaking her by the shoulders to get her to wake up. His eyes danced from her to Ray. The way he looked at her wasn't something she was used to seeing. He was afraid. Afraid of what she would have done if he hadn't stopped her. Ruby looked down at her own shaking hands. The power in them still tingling, begging her to use it again. She shoved her fists into her jacket pocket, hiding them from the world.

"We need to get a cab and get her to the center before she wakes up," she said, and lead the way back towards the street.

She could hear Liam pick up Ray and follow her out. His footsteps loud and determined. She had no doubt he'd be speaking to her about what happened when they got back. "Let's hope she wakes up in the first place." He said as they stepped into the brightly lit street.

CHAPTER 22
TROUBLE WITH SELF-CONTROL

"The fog, how did you make it appear?" Ruby asked, leaning over the chair Ray was tied to. They had been taking turns questioning her for hours without any luck and Ruby was slowly losing her patience. "Listen, I know you're probably scared but we're not going to hurt you."

Ray's laugh echoed in the room making her sound like an evil villain in a movie. "If you think I'm scared then you're a bigger idiot than I thought."

"Oh, look at that! It speaks!" Liam yelled out sarcastically.

"Why did you try to steal my necklace? For money? Why?" Ruby started to raise her voice. She was just about done with this girl's attitude.

"We don't want your money, fool."

"We? Who's we?"

Now we're getting somewhere, Ruby thought. But as soon as her hopes were up, they were back to square one. Ray was as silent now as when they first brought her in. She pushed her face closer to Ray, forcing her to make eye contact.

"I said, who's we?" she yelled. Her hands steaming with rage, burning through the chair handles she was pressing on. "You had better stop wasting my time!"

"Hey. Let's all just take a breather for a minute," Liam's hand was on her shoulder now, pulling her away and trying to calm her down, "let's get a coffee really quick." He pulled her back firmly, letting her know this wasn't up for debate.

Ruby pushed herself back up and started to follow him out of the room. A part of her wanted to stay. To push Ray harder, get some sort of answers. But she knew with her powers acting out, things could only get worse. What if she couldn't control herself again and hurt this girl? Or worse, what if she hurt someone in the center. Liam was right, she needed a break.

"Having some trouble with self-control, are we?" she heard Ray yell out behind them.

Her hand reached for Liam's immediately knowing he was the only thing that could calm her down. If this girl kept pressing her luck, she'd regret it. "What do you think she meant by that?" She asked when they were out of the room.

"She'd just being a tool. Trying to get under your skin."

"Yeah, I guess you're right," she smiled, but something about it didn't sit well. Ray knew something, she could feel it. She was connected to the thefts, the sword, to all of it. And now more than ever Ruby was sure she was also connected to her.

CHAPTER 23
HER FRIEND WAS GONE

The walk back to her apartment was exhausting. She had somehow persuaded Liam not to go back with her, knowing that she needed some time alone to gather her thoughts. By the time she finally reached home, she was regretting her decision not to take him up on his offer. Her mind was still as jumbled as it had been at the center, and now she was missing him as well.

She inched her way up the stairs, hoping Shaylah would be home and willing to hang out.

As she pushed the door open, she could hear Shaylah laughing with someone in the living room.

Ah crap! She thought, *does she have a date here?*

Making sure to make a lot of noise, she dropped her keys on the table in the hall and threw her bag forcefully on the floor.

"Hey, Fish! You're home early!" Shaylah yelled from the couch.

"Yeah, just needed some time to relax and... oh..." her eyes noticed the other person on the couch, "I didn't you were coming by, Jake."

Jake rearranged his glasses and leaned towards the coffee table to grab a drink. He was acting as if she wasn't even in the room, a lack of interest she hadn't seen in him since the one time they had a fight in grade two. "Wasn't planned or anything. I ran into Shay down the street."

"We were just about to go catch a movie. You want to come, Fish?" Shaylah's hands pressed together into a begging motion, "The three of us haven't hung out in, like, forever!"

She looked at Jake, wishing for some semblance of interest on his part. An invitation for her to join them, to repair their friendship. But his eyes stared blankly into his cup, looking as bored as ever. Her friend was gone and she wasn't sure if she would ever get him back again. "It's okay, Shay. You guys go. I'm so beat I'd probably fall asleep halfway through."

"You sure? It's some garbage horror like you like?"

"Yeah, I'm sure. You guys have fun though!"

She walked briskly into her room, closing the door behind her and sinking into her bed. Her heart was in pieces. She wanted nothing more than to share her stories from the day with Jake. To get stared at by strangers when they laughed during the scary parts of a bad movie. She wanted him back in her life the way he used to be, before she messed everything up.

Tears pooled in her eyes, making them look darker than they were. As she fell asleep, she thought only of regret and disappointment, and her dreams that night were filled with vivid images of her own shortcomings. Of all the ways she wasn't the girl they all expected her to be.

CHAPTER 24
SOMETHING DARKER

Cold sweat covered Ruby's body when she woke up. Her bed was soaked and she couldn't wait to get up and take a shower. Her eyes opened wearily, trying to get adjusted to the darkness in her room. What time was it? She couldn't tell, it was much too dark to already be morning. Something about the blackness of the night felt unnatural. There was usually some light shining through her bedroom window, but at this moment, she couldn't see a thing.

"Shay?" she yelled out, hoping she wasn't alone in the apartment. No response.

She started to get up but couldn't move. Something was holding her down. Her heart rose to a panicked state, beating like it was planning to rip right through her. She pushed herself up again, this time feeling a sharp pain in her wrists and legs. She was tied down; someone had tied her down!

Her body slashed in the bed, kicking against the restraints.

"Hel...!" she started to yell but her voice was silenced before the scream could leave her lips. Her head spun left and right, trying to see what was happening to her.

As her eyes gained some focus, she looked ahead in horror. At the edge of her bed, dark figures stood in a line. She could count about five of them. As dark as the fog she summoned when she tapped into her Aether-Born powers. She tried to scream again without so much as a whimper coming through. It was a familiar feeling, she had had it before when Elena ran her drills with her. Someone here had sucked the voice right out of her.

The figures were blurred, covered from her vision by something that wouldn't stop moving.

Black fog! She thought, this time realizing the true danger of the situation. *Is this another vision?*

Her hand wiggled but the more she moved, the tighter the restraints got, cutting into her flesh like a million razors. She could feel a cold, metallic pull on her with each cut. Was she chained down? She couldn't see in the dark but she was willing to bet her life on it.

Ruby tried to breathe slower, to root herself deep inside of her thoughts, powering herself up. Nothing. Not even as much as smoke came off her.

Whispers surrounded her. Not sentences, something darker. Like a quiet beat of a drum made of words she didn't understand. She tried to will herself to create a fire, at least enough to reassure herself, but every time her body was about to connect with her Elemental emotions, she only sank deeper into the bed. Into her own cold sweat.

Tears flooded her eyes, rushing down her cheeks and onto her neck. She needed to find a way out of this. Thinking back to her training she tried to remember anything that Liam might have taught her that would help in this mess. She could try to dislocate her thumb and free one of her hands. But then what? It was five to one and she had a feeling she'd lose this fight with only one able hand to protect her.

I'm screwed.

As she ran through escape scenarios, her face froze, staring above her. Suspended in mid-air a dark fog started to take human shape. Materializing from nothing and getting darker by the second. She pushed into the bed instinctively, away from whatever danger floated just inches from her. The dark figure was less like fog now, still as fluid but thick like molasses. A drop fell from it, landing on her forehead. She winced from the sharp pain of the drop as it scorched her skin. Burning into her flesh in a searing drip.

Is this what the vision was? Is this how I die?

CHAPTER 25
THE WORST OF IT

The liquid from the creature forming above her oozed down her body, burning her pale skin with every touch. She wanted to crawl out of her skin. She wanted to scream. She wanted to hurt it back the same way it was hurting her.

"Get the hell away from her!" A voice sounded from her bedroom door and a ball of fire shot through the figure above her.

Liam!

The fire did nothing to physically hurt the creature but it did cause it to startle. Whatever grip it had on her vanished for a brief second giving Ruby enough time to reach her powers. Her skin lit into flames, melting the chains that held her. She sat up in her bed, brushing off the molten metal rapidly. When she looked at her arms and legs, she could see black veins covering them—

moving inside her like her blood was turning into the same darkness the creature was made of.

"Liam! The others!" She screamed, pointing at the dark figures at the edge of the bed.

His hands moved quickly, forming a blazing wall of fire between the figures and the edge of the bed. He rushed to her side, helping her get to her feet so they could make their way out of the room. When she started to stand up, she could feel something reach for the back of her neck. A stinging, hotness grasped her, pulling her back towards it.

She pushed Liam out of the way and spun around towards the creature that was trying to drag her back. Her hands moved with her, pushing the air away from her and directing it towards her attacker. A black fog trailed behind her.

The first hit knocked it back, causing it to slide in the air away from her. "This one's going to hurt!" She screamed and pushed another line of fog towards it. Every emotion in her body pushed out of her hands, she didn't just want to hurt it, she wanted to kill it.

The creature stumbled back, shaking off the pain. It looked like it was about to charge at her. Ruby widened her stance, she could feel Liam's heat at her back, ready to fight alongside her. She pushed her hands out but just as she was about to charge, the figure vanished.

They stood back to back, circling around the room, trying to see where to point their attacks but it was empty. The figures had vanished just as quickly as they had appeared. Ruby bent over, she felt like she was going to throw up. "What the hell was that?" she asked, knowing that Liam had just as many answers as she did.

"Are you okay? Let me see your face," Liam said, spinning her around to him and examining every inch of her body, "I thought we were done for sure."

"Liam, what was that thing? Who were those people? What was that *thing*?" She had so many questions her head was starting to spin. Her legs buckled under her and she fell into Liam's side.

"Whoa! Okay let's get you down here for a second," He helped her to the bed, letting her rest her body on his chest, "Have you ever seen anything like that before?"

"Seriously? You honestly think this is something I could have seen... and just, like, what? Shrugged it off like it's nothing? Oh, just another creepy, foggy, creature trying to kill me, no big deal."

"Okay, I get it. Just thought maybe you'd read about it or something."

"No, I haven't read about it. I still don't even understand how *it* and those other freaks got in here. And why they were here in the first place."

She was trying to make sense of what just happened. Going through the night step by step to see if something made it clearer for her but there was no sense in any of it. Why were they after her? It couldn't have been the sword pieces; her necklace was on the entire time and no one tried to steal it. What were those people chanting? Why couldn't she use her powers?

Ruby had so many questions, she wanted to rush back to the center right away and start looking for answers. What had they missed that could explain all of this? Throughout the entire attack, she felt she was in danger but there was something else she felt that she couldn't quite put her finger on. There had to be more to it than just hurting her. That thing wanted something from her, but what? If she didn't even know what it was, how was she supposed to protect herself?

"What are you doing here anyway?" she asked.

"I called you. About twenty times or so. When you didn't answer, I figured I should check on you, just in case. Plus, I kind of wanted to see you again," He smiled and pulled her in closer, "the center is just not the same when you're not there."

"Liam?" she looked up into his green eyes, losing herself almost entirely for a moment.

"What's up?"

"You think this is what my vision was about?"

"I really hope so."

She pulled away from him, taken back by the response. She was trying to find some humor in his face but he was as serious as ever. "What? Why?"

"Because if this was your vision, at least we know what it was about and that it's done and over with now. Yes, we will have to figure out why it all happened but for now, at least we don't need to worry what your vision meant," he wrapped his arms around her and pulled them both to the bed. "We can worry about it tomorrow. Try to close your eyes for a minute."

"I doubt I can sleep right now. What if they come back?"

"We'll be fine, Rue. They won't be back tonight. It looked like you did a bit of damage on that thing in the end there. And you need your strength if we're going to figure this out. Trust me, the worst of it all is behind us."

She let him press her into his chest, feeling every toned muscle against her face, rocking her into a dreamless stupor. She knew she should get some rest, he was right about that, but there was one thing Liam was dead wrong about. They hadn't seen the worst of it yet. That she was sure of.

CHAPTER 26
THEY CALLED HER EIRENE

"So, you guys actually found something in these?" Ruby gestured at her grandmother's journals, surprised that someone was actually able to make sense of the gibberish on the pages.

Alice walked over to Ruby's side carrying one of the journals. She put the book in front of her and rested a hand on her shoulder, rubbing it gently. Ruby had a feeling that after yesterday's attack, everyone was going to walk on eggshells around her. She hated the idea of the elders thinking she needed their protection. She was the one who was supposed to be looking after them. Some leader she was.

"Girl, are you ok?" Leah's bubbly voice broke the silence, "Like, after yesterday I mean?"

Ruby looked up at her and stifled a laugh. Leave it to Leah to see the elephant in the room and draw more attention to it. After that comment, the elephant might as well be wearing a floral cap and dancing the tango. "Everything is fine. Just tell me what you guys found here."

"Not us actually, Myriam and Harvey are to thank for that," Alice said.

"Oh, cool," she was wondering where the two were right now and why they wouldn't be here to break the news of their discovery, "I'll have to thank them later, I guess."

"Of course, I'm sure they wanted to be here but you know, with the preparations..."

How could she forget, they'd been spending every free moment getting everything ready for Liam's parents. If she didn't know better, she'd think the Pope himself was paying them a visit. Myriam and Harvey had spent the better half of the week going over every detail in the center. Driving everyone crazy with advice on what they should and shouldn't do when the Nars arrive. Ruby was definitely sick of it. "Right," she said, and rolled her eyes, "So, what's in here exactly?"

Alice opened the book to one of the pages clearly marked by a blue post-it note. Someone had spent some time color coding these. She could see Leah beaming with pride when she saw her notice the post-it. Of course, it had to be her, no one else cared this much about organization.

"See this mark here?" She pointed at one of the

drawings in the journal that looked like a circle with two crossed lines beneath it, "It kept popping up randomly throughout the journals. Myriam found out it's an ancient symbol for the underworld."

"What does that have to do with AetherBorns?" Ruby asked in confusion.

"Exactly! Nothing!"

"I'm not following here, Alice."

"The symbol isn't one of the elements so it wouldn't have anything to do with the AetherBorns or the Elementals which made us wonder why it was there. They started going through some of the mythology books here that aren't specific to Elementals and that's when they found it."

"Found what? You're really stretching this out." Ruby's brow furrowed; she was really hoping they would get to the point soon.

"The symbol! They found the symbol! It was used to identify the underworld, also known as Tartarus back in the day."

"But Tartarus is also one of the original deities!" Leah shouted, "Sorry, spoiler alert."

"Yes, very good. Anyhow, we started doing some more research on him and found an old legend that tells of a time when Tartarus was tired of being a deity and hid from the other Gods on Earth. It's believed that while he was here, he fell in love with an extraordinary woman who possessed powers beyond those of anyone else in this world. They called her Eirene."

"The original AetherBorn..." Ruby whispered.

"The one and only," Leah joined in, "But, oh my God! It gets so much better!"

Alice gave Leah a pointed look that meant she needed to stay quiet, and as much as Ruby loved her commentaries, she wanted to hear the rest of the story. "So, the girl that Eirene gave birth to was, what? His?"

"It seems to be so. The other Gods found out about the union, and to punish Tartarus for his interference on Earth, created a place under Hades made of pure darkness, and banished him into that prison. It's said that the underworld is actually called Tartarus after him, which is why it was so hard to find information. Everything we read could be interpreted two ways."

"Did you find anything else?"

"This was as far as we got. Some of the history gets mixed up in different books."

"So, that's all we have?"

"Ruby, you must understand how difficult it is to dig this information up. Your grandmother's journals were a good start but it's not as if the history of the Aether-Borns gets passed down through generations. Your father is born into the lineage and he knows very little about this himself. I'm sure you can imagine that we know even less considering that for the longest time, we thought the AetherBorn line had become extinct. I mean, the last one died in some freak accident before my own grandmother was an elder. We're running on fumes when it comes to finding things out about your kind."

"I know, I'm sorry. I didn't mean to offend you." She felt like a jerk for her unnecessary attitude, "You guys did great finding all of this. It's a lot more than we had before. I just wish there was something here that could help us find out more about who took the sword pieces."

"Well, actually, there is something else."

"What?"

"In all of your grandmother's journals there are two repeating words over and over. She mentions the sword in many of her notes on her visions, but also the word 'gate'."

"Gate? What kind of gate?"

"That's exactly what we were wondering, too. Whatever this gate opens, we are certain that the sword plays a big part."

Ruby's face tightened. How could they know so little about something that could be a danger to their entire species? If Alice was right and the sword was needed to open some gate, whoever is stealing the sword pieces knows more about the AetherBorns than they themselves did, which made them a very dangerous enemy. She needed to get more answers and fast, with two pieces gone, who's to say they wouldn't attack again soon to get the rest of them? Ruby was done playing games, she had to do whatever she could to protect them all.

"I need to see the alley girl," she got up to walk away.

Leah chased after her with worry flooding her face. Her concern was touching, Leah was the closest to a sister that she'd ever had. She hated making her worry, but they were out of options. "Are you sure it's such a good idea? Last time you had that whole thing with your powers."

"She's the only one who might be able to tell us who's behind this, and I'm going to make her talk no matter what it takes. If anyone has any better ideas, you know where to find me."

Her words were full of fury and finality. Leah stood back in the room and let the door close behind Ruby's receding steps, she wasn't one to interfere with her superior's decisions.

CHAPTER 27
SO MANY QUESTIONS

"**A**re you sure you want to do this?" Liam chased after her down the hall, "Remember last time?"

"I'm sure. I'll keep my shit together."

"And if you can't?"

"She's not going to talk to anyone else. She knows something, I can feel it. That fog she created wasn't just a coincidence. Tell me you haven't thought so, too?"

"I have. Obviously."

"There's only one explanation for it. She has to be an AetherBorn. Like me."

"But why would another AetherBorn be after the sword? It just makes no sense. And how did we not know there're more of them out there?"

"That's exactly what I'm planning to find out."

They stood in front of the room holding Ray

hostage. She could feel her emotions fizzing inside her. Every time she was around this girl something in her screamed to get out. This must be what was making her powers act out this entire time, ever since she first met Ray, it was as if parts of her that lay dormant before were creeping to the surface. She didn't exactly have a lot to go by, her powers were as new to everyone else as they had been to her, but since Ray showed up, she was all over the place. More so than usual, at least. "Liam, she's the answer to all of this. I know it."

"Just promise me you won't do anything stupid."

"I promise." She said and opened the door, "But just in case, get ready to help me out."

Ray's eyes flashed to her as soon as she walked in. She watched her every move, smiling. "I knew you'd be back, princess."

"I don't have time for your games."

"Oh, but I love games. You have Monopoly?" she laughed.

"How do you have AetherBorn powers? You look way too young to have gotten the call."

"Not all of us are late bloomers like you and your grams, Miss Black," Ray joked, "Maybe we're just stronger than you are."

She could see the girl's face change, proud like she had won some competition. But Ruby knew better. She used the word 'we,' that meant there were more Aether-Born out there. Ray messed up; she had her now. "So, there're more of you?" she asked, watching Ray's arrogance drop. Despite the attitude, she was still just a kid and Ruby almost felt sorry for her. That is until she remembered the knife stab this kid left her with before.

"I'm done talking to you," she turned her head away defiantly.

Liam walked towards her, cupping her face in his hands and turning her back to face Ruby. "I don't think so, kid."

"Why do you need the sword pieces? You're supposed to be a protector! Why are you not working with us? Why hide and steal when we're clearly on the same side?" She was shouting at her now, her mouth almost frothing with each word that she spat in Ray's direction. The words coated her like venomous dust sprinkled on a poisonous cake.

Ray's eyes squinted. Hatred washing over them with the force of a dam breaking. She blew her bangs out of her face, shaking Liam's hands away. Her body straightened and she sharpened her gaze on Ruby. She looked less like a kid now and more like a feral animal. "You think we're the same?" She shrieked, "All you want to do is protect your precious little Elementals! They're the reason your grams killed herself and you're still trying to help them! You're an idiot!"

"My grandmother killed herself because no one believed her."

"And why do you think that is? She never even had

a chance to meet others like her. For the Elementals, we're just some dirty little secret that they'd rather wash away. You think if you hadn't stopped them from killing each other they'd ever let you step foot in their world?" Her words pierced through Ruby, "The only reason you're on their side is because you don't know anything about who you really are."

"So, tell me. Tell me what you know and help me understand."

"You'll never understand. You're not like us. You never will be. Just give up, you'll never win this."

"Win what? What exactly are you planning?"

"Do you really think I'm that dumb? We can have these little chit chats all you want, but you're not getting anything out of me. I'm not some weakling girl playing Elemental dress up like you."

Ruby could feel the rage in her bubbling to the surface. Her entire body was convulsing with energy. Her hands formed into fists and her jaw clenched so tightly she wasn't sure it would open again. Fog formed at her fingertips, slowly creeping towards Ray. The darkness of it wrapped around her ankles, curling its blurred edges up her legs.

"Oh, look who's a big, bad AetherBorn, now?" Ray teased.

Ruby tried to breathe, she tried to calm down and lower her guard. But no matter what she tried, the fog became denser, rushing up Ray's body. Ready to devour her. It swirled around the seated girl, ripping through her, beating her from the inside out. Ruby watched her writhe and thrash, smiling as she twisted the fog tighter around her chest.

She was still smiling when Liam jumped in between her and Ray. His hands outstretched, threatening to burn if she didn't back down. She wanted to get him out of the way but in order to do so she would need to hurt him, too. Her hands relaxed, letting the fog disperse into the air.

There was still so much more she needed to get out of this girl. So many questions that Ray could answer. Why had Liam interrupted her? Was she the only one who understood how important all of this was?

Without another word, she turned on her heels and walked out of the room, glancing back at Ray's slouched body as she left. "Maybe next time you'll make this easier on yourself," she said, and let the door slam behind her.

CHAPTER 28
HIS DARKNESS IS A PART OF ME

"You want to explain what the hell happened in there?" Liam cried out as they walked towards his room.

"She knew things, you saw that."

"What I saw was you get pissed and lose your temper. Again."

"But she has answers! Answers that we need right now!"

He grabbed her elbow, stopping her in her tracks. "That is not how we get them," he said and pulled her closer. She leaned her back on the wall and let herself slide down to the floor. What was happening to her? What was she turning into? She felt as though something opened in her. Something dark that wanted to get out, to hurt people. Something hungry for power and blood. This wasn't who she wanted to be but what if succumbing to this darkness is what she needed to do to save them all? To save Liam?

"I'm scared," she whispered, "I don't know what's happening to me."

"Rue, you know I have your back, right? I would do anything for you, but this, we can't be these people. We can't become..." he stopped.

"Become what, Liam? Say it."

"Evil. We can't become evil."

"What if I don't have a choice."

"What are you talking about?"

She thought about how good it felt to hurt Ray. The rush of power through her, the control over whether or not someone lives or dies. But it wasn't Ray she was picturing in that chair when she used her powers. It might have been Ray's body paying the price, but it was Cyril's face staring back at her. He was the one she pictured tied down and having the life crushed out of him. Payment for everything he did before the treaty that made her life a living hell. For killing Liam. "Did Alice tell you what they found out about my lineage?"

"Leah did, yeah."

"What if his darkness is a part of me somehow? A part of all AetherBorns?"

"I highly doubt that. Besides, we don't know the guy was evil."

"That *guy* was a God, Liam. One of the originals.

They made a special hell place just for him, doesn't sound like he's the greatest."

"It's just a legend, Rue. You can't decide who you are based on a legend." He reached his arm around her shoulders, pulling her into a hug, "Besides, you're one of the kindest people I've ever met. If it wasn't for you, all of us Elementals would still be running around trying to kill each other for the sword. Or did you forget that part?"

"I don't know," she shrugged.

"Well, I do. There is nothing dark about you, Rue. Everyone gets angry sometimes. Besides, I think you're pretty hot when you're mad, so..."

She laughed and nudged his side and was about to pull him in for a kiss, when a voice boomed through the speakers in the hallway.

"Great news everyone! The Nars have finally made it back to Westerlake. Come join us in the cafeteria for a warm welcome to our most beloved family!" Harvey and Myriam sang in unison.

Liam looked over at her, waiting for some hint of excitement and she was surprised that in the midst of all of this, he still had the hope of them acting like a regular couple. She forced a smile to her face and jumped up to her feet.

"Let's get this over with," she said, and pulled him up next to her.

CHAPTER 29

LIAM HAS TOLD US SO MUCH ABOUT YOU!

The cafeteria was full of people and chatter, Ruby couldn't believe how many people came by to say hello to Liam's parents. The center lit up as though a celebrity was gracing its halls with their presence. All around her, Elementals were laughing, having drinks and participating in their chatter. Almost like there wasn't some big threat looming over them.

She clutched Liam's hand in a death-grip as they made their way past the groups of people towards the Nars. The sweat of her palms threatened to make their hands slide away from each but she tightened her grip. The closer they got, the more her nerves rushed through her body. If she didn't get this out of the way soon, she was definitely going to pass out. She felt Liam let go of her hand to run towards his parents, leaving her standing alone in her own wreck of emotions. When he got a chance to say hello, he gestured for her to come join them.

"And this is Ruby." He said pointing in her direction, "The girl I told you about."

She reached a reluctant, clammy hand to his dad. Steadying herself for an awkward handshake. To her surprise, his father pushed her hand out of the way and pulled her in for a hug. "It's great to finally meet you, Ruby!" He exclaimed in a tone that made it sound like he had been waiting to meet her his entire life.

"Oh, Liam, she is a beauty!" His mom declared and rushed towards her, "How are you, dear? Liam has told us so much about you!"

Ruby turned her eyes to Liam, wondering exactly what he had told them so far.

"Yep! That's her all right!" His hand reached for hers and she grabbed it desperately.

"It's nice to meet you, Mr. and Mrs. Nars." She said, "How was the flight here?"

"Oh, honey! Sebastian and Abigail are just fine!" Liam's mom sang, her voice as gentle as that of a fairy-tale princess.

Ruby studied the two of them. She could see Liam's resemblance in his dad. The same green eyes and dark hair. Even the same build, except Liam was a bit more muscular and filled out. His mom, on the other hand, was nothing like him. She was slim, almost too slim, with long blonde hair tied into a high bun. She reminded Ruby of a Hollywood housewife in the way she carried herself, regal and long, nothing like the casual stance of Liam and his father.

"Oh, you absolutely must meet Trudie!" she yelled out and pulled Ruby towards one of the tables.

"Sure! Who's Trudie?" she asked Liam quietly.

"The dog," he laughed, and followed the two of them.

Ruby didn't even have time to turn around before Abigail shoved a tiny, shaking Chihuahua into her arms. The poor thing looked hilarious in her little pink jacket and Ruby couldn't help but let out a giggle. "Hi, Trudie." She waved at the dog cheerfully.

"Don't bother," Sebastian noted behind her, "she can't see a thing."

"Oh. Sorry."

"Don't worry about it, she's pretty old." Liam tried to make her feel less uncomfortable, "Mom treats her better than me and dad."

"Listen, you two," his dad stood between them with an arm around both her and Liam, "we have a few more people to say hello to, but what do you say once we get settled in we all go out for dinner? Get to know each other better? I can't wait to hear about everything that's been happening here!"

He put his hand on Abigail's back and led her towards Myriam and Harvey who looked like they could not be happier to speak to them. She pushed a deep breathe out, finally relaxing. As far as meeting the parents goes, this wasn't the worst.

"See," Liam said, "that wasn't so bad."

"You could have warned me about Trudie."

"Yeah, she's like a permanent fixture in our house, I seriously forget somet..."

"Guys! You need to come quick!" Zag's red, shaggy hair pushed in between them. He was pulling on Ruby's arm and had her a few feet away from Liam already who was running behind them, struggling to catch up.

"Zag! What is going on?" she yelled.

"Something happened. You need to come with me."

She had no idea what the urgency was but his tone sounded serious. Letting him drag her, she turned around to make sure Liam was still behind them. She was still wondering what had happened when she realized where they were going.

Zag was taking her to the room where Ray was being held.

CHAPTER 30
THIS JUST DOESN'T MAKE SENSE

Ruby didn't need to ask what happened when they walked into the room. She knew exactly why Zag was in a panic to get them here. A nauseated knot formed in her stomach as she got closer to the chair. She looked closely at Ray's lifeless body. Her arms hanging at her side and her head slumped forward. The deep purple of her hair covering her face entirely.

"Omg!" Leah yelled from the doorway, "is she dead?"

Liam walked past her, kneeling down next to the girl and putting two fingers behind her ear. He waited a few seconds then turned to Ruby, fear in his eyes. "She's definitely dead."

"How did this happen?" Ruby said, defeated, "How

could anyone get in here? I thought we had someone watching her at all times."

"We did! I was right outside the door!" Zag's voice raised, and she could see he felt guilty about what happened. She knew it wasn't his fault, but couldn't help but be a little pissed that it happened on his watch.

"And you didn't see anyone come in?"

"Of course not! You think I'm just going to let someone in, no problem?"

"Well, they got in somehow. Is there another way they could have gotten inside? Some window we don't know about?"

"We're underground, Rue." Liam said quietly.

"Right. This just doesn't make sense."

She paced around the room trying to find a point of entrance they might have missed. There was only one explanation for how someone got inside and they were not going to like it. Hell, she didn't like it. "It had to have been an AetherBorn."

"Why? If it was someone Ray worked with, why would they kill her?"

"I don't know. Maybe she wasn't useful to them anymore, or maybe they we were worried she might start talking. But it's the only thing that would make any sense. No one else could get in here."

"But how would they even get inside?"

"You can teleport by using fire, maybe they can do the same with the black fog?" The word left a bad taste on her lips as it escaped. *They.* If *they* could move from place to place using the fog, did that mean she could, too? What else could they do that Ruby knew nothing about? What could *she* do? She felt like a shell of herself, there was still so much about her powers that she didn't know. The thought made her feel weak and useless and she hated that.

"Couldn't it be another Fire Elemental then?"

"I doubt it. There'd be burn marks somewhere that we'd see." Zag offered, "When I came in to check on her, the room was completely untouched."

"Guys?" Ruby said, and walked towards Ray's body, "Do you see that?"

"See what?" Liam asked, peering over her shoulders to understand what she meant.

"That," Ruby said, and pulled the hair out of Ray's face, revealing her eyes.

She heard Leah's gasp behind them and her own heart jumped at what she was seeing. Ray's eyes were the same black as they were in the alley when she attacked, but this time the darkness oozed like tears down her face. Ruby reached a finger to one of the drips and pulled away quickly.

"Ow!" She yelped at the burning pain on her fingertip, "We have a huge problem."

CHAPTER 31
A PLAN

She was perched cross legged on one of the tables in the greenhouse. Her head was throbbing from over-thinking. Every thought and every question she had had since they found Ray pulsated in her mind, burning their urgency into her. Her finger danced back and forth on top of a sprout, making it mimic her movements. Connecting to the plants was something she tended to do when she was deep in thought. The energy needed to move them was minimal and it made her feel like she was breathing life into them, doing something useful for a change.

"Rue, what are you thinking?" Liam asked. He had been crouched beside her this entire time but she had barely said one word to him.

"I don't know." She said, meeting his eyes. "Everything is such a mess."

"None of this is your fault. You know that, right?"

"Isn't it? Ray was AetherBorn, like me. Technically, that makes her family."

"And?"

"And someone out there killed her. Probably another AetherBorn, or whatever that *thing* was that tried to hurt me. I mean, yes, she was an ass but I didn't want her dead."

"Because she had information?"

She looked at him, hurt curling the corners of her mouth downward. She couldn't believe this is why he thought she wanted Ray alive. What did he think of her? Worse, how was she behaving lately that made him think this? His words struck her like a slap in the face inviting a duel. They made her fear what she may be turning into. "No, not because she had information. Because she was a person. A person I was related to somehow."

"Right," he held her hand apologetically, "Take it from someone who has had his share of family drama, just because you're related, doesn't mean you're family."

Ruby let his words sink in, wondering who he was talking about. As far as she could tell, Liam's family seemed great. Sure, they'd left him alone to fight with the resistance but what would they have done even if they'd stayed? Liam was definitely able to take care of himself. She made a mental note to press him about it some other time, right now she needed to figure out a plan. "So, this thing from the other night." She said, changing the subject, "What if it is also AetherBorn? Some dark version of one or something?"

"Is this about you being dark or evil again? Because, I thought we agreed you're not going to stress about that?"

His hand went to hug her but she slapped it away.

"No, it's not about *that*! It's about what we do next."

"Oh." He was clearly hurt by her reaction, but she didn't have time to deal with a bruised ego, at the moment. Lives were on the line.

"We need to be ready for the next attack. I think it's safe to say that we both know they're not stopping any time soon. At least not until they get the all the sword pieces." Her hand rubbed the Onyx necklace instinctively, "If there are more AetherBorns out there and if they're being led by someone, we need to be ready. We'll need to find her, their leader."

"That's a lot of ifs."

"Well, that's all we have right now. We have to consider all the possibilities."

"Ok. So, either you're right, and there are more AetherBorns who want the sword, or you're wrong, and Ray was just a misguided kid who knew too much about things she didn't understand."

"Yep. If I'm wrong, that still doesn't explain who killed her and how."

Liam crossed his legs and put his face in his palms.

His brows drawn in concentration, like he was trying to catch a thought just in the front of his mind. "But if there are more of them, we still don't know what they want with the sword."

"Right."

"There is another option, too."

"Which is?"

"That whatever it was that attacked you, somehow had nothing to do with you or AetherBorns. Maybe there's some other reason the sword is important."

She thought about it for a second. They had no actual evidence that pointed to other AetherBorns existing. It's not like there was some phone directory or a family tree she could check. As far as the black fog that Ray created went, no one could say for sure that the power was reserved for AetherBorns. The girl wasn't exactly forthcoming with information. Ruby herself had all the powers of the Elementals, maybe there was an Elemental out there that had more powers than they knew about.

Her eyes flicked to the door. She had the strangest feeling that they were being watched. She looked around the greenhouse but saw nothing except the slight wavering of plant leaves. She could have sworn she saw movement before. She rubbed her eyes, realizing that what she needed was to get some sleep. All of this was starting to wear down on her. Liam watched her closely, creases of concern forming on his brow. She'd better say something before he asked her to explain why she was acting odd. "Could be," she quickly offered, "but something about it just didn't seem right. I know I'm probably jumping to conclusions here, but whatever that creature was, I was connected to it somehow. Same way as I was to Ray. Did you feel anything around it?"

"Just that I wanted to kick its ass for hurting you," he said, smiling.

"Okay, see? I'm the only one that felt it. That has to mean something."

"Fine. Say you're completely right and there's some secret army of AetherBorns that are trying to get the sword and they're led by some super leader girl. Then what? All the information we have about your lineage is buried in legends and tales. How do we even fight that?"

"Well, that's not *all* we have..." She said, "We have me."

She watched his face go from confused to completely dumbfounded. She knew how this sounded. How could a girl who had just found out she was AetherBorn a short while ago help gather information on a lineage that lay secret for hundreds of years? "I'm an AetherBorn, right?" she said, trying to explain it to him.

"Uh huh..."

"So, I must have the same powers as they all do, right?"

"Yeah..." He still wasn't getting it.

"Well, if we find a way to figure out *all* of my powers, we can know how to prepare for any attack they might send our way. We just need to start testing things to see how many powers I can tap into."

"Yes! That way whatever they try to send our way, we'll know how to thwart it!"

Finally, she thought. *Welcome to the party.*

"But it can't be just me. Everyone has to be ready to fight. We don't know how many of them there are and what we can expect when they make their move. Every single Elemental has to be ready."

"They will be. We'll make sure of it."

"And Liam?"

"Yeah?"

"I want my parents to get trained, too. They might not have powers, but my dad is part of the AetherBorn line. If they're looking to hurt me, he's definitely a target. They need to be able to protect themselves if anything happens."

"Of course. We'll get them to come stay here for a bit. Just to be safe."

"Great." She looked back at the sprout next to her. How still it was when she wasn't forcing her powers into it. Like everyone else in her life, it was at peace until she came along with all her baggage. Her eyes suddenly flashed to Liam's, realizing something she hadn't thought of before. "You realize that means our parents will have to meet, right?"

"Well... we've been through worse..." he laughed, but she could hear the nervous galloping of his voice in each note.

CHAPTER 32
THEY WILL PAY

Ruby walked down the stairs of the pawn shop entrance towards a massive crowd of people. She was trying to figure out what she had to say, but more importantly, her every thought concentrated on not tripping or doing anything else foolish. The elders did a great job at getting every Elemental to come out, a little too great a job for Ruby's liking. Her nerves were starting to get the better of her. She had never been good at public speaking, and now with lives at stake, she had a feeling she would forget every word she'd practiced saying. Liam was right, she should have just winged it.

As she stepped down a few more steps, her eyes found her parents in the crowd. They looked so out of place here, but somehow had already managed to make a few friends. They were chit chatting with Zag's parents when Cyril and Rhea walked up to them. Ruby could see her dad's back stiffen up, whatever pleasantries they exchanged were awkward at best, and she was glad to see them part ways quickly. With the twisted way in which her relationship with Jake was unfolding, she could suddenly relate to her dad's feelings towards Cyril. She was starting to develop the same distaste for his son, after the way he'd started treating her. When she found out about her family's past, she thought that their parents' hatred for each other had something to do with their AetherBorn bloodline, and Cyril wanting to stay in control of the Elementals. Now, she was starting to wonder if maybe that wasn't it at all. Maybe the Okenos family was simply so drenched in self-assurance that they couldn't help but push everyone away. As if on cue, she spotted Jake in the crowd, and turned her head defiantly away from him. He was definitely not the Elemental she wanted to see right now. In fact, she had somebody very different on her mind.

Her eyes scanned the crowd. *Where is he?* She moved from face to face, finally finding him in the front row. His eyes burning through her heart as he watched her descend. Liam brushed his hair back and gave her a quick wink making her almost lose her balance. *Get it together! You're supposed to set an example,* she thought and got ready to speak.

"Uhm. Hi, everyone. Thanks for coming out. I know

you all probably have better things to do on a Saturday..." her voice trailed off, and she started getting dizzy.

She looked at Liam again, wishing he was up here with her. "You got this." He mouthed as if sensing her nerves.

"Anyway. I'm sure you're wondering why you're here. I asked the elders to get everyone together because there have been some things happening, and I don't think it's right that you're all kept in the dark." She saw Cyril's face tense but kept going, "There has been two sword pieces stolen from us. Two pieces that were heavily guarded." Whispers shot through the crowd. Everyone was on edge; she could feel it. "And there's something else. There might be other AetherBorns out there. We think they might be responsible. Well... *I* think."

"What? How is that even possible?" someone yelled out, but she couldn't make out the voice.

"We don't really know, yet. But we know that they will be coming for the rest of the sword pieces. Probably very soon. We had one of them captured, but yesterday someone broke into the center and..." She paused, her heart breaking, "The AetherBorn was killed."

There was silence for what seemed like hours. In truth, only a few seconds passed, but to Ruby it felt like an eternity. "So, what the hell do we now? Just wait until they take us out one by one?" another member yelled out, and all eyes turned to Ruby, waiting for her response.

"This is why I wanted everyone to come here. We're not going to sit around and wait for someone to come into our center and take what's ours. We need to be ready. Everyone needs to be ready. We will train, every day if that's what it takes, but when..." She took a breath and steadied herself, "If they come back, we will put a stop to it."

"Aren't you supposed to keep the sword safe? That's the whole point of this treaty isn't it?"

Her eyes moved through the people, trying to find who said that. Who was making it harder for her to stand here than it already was? 'The point of her' is what they meant to say and she knew it. It's not that she didn't understand their fear, just that there was no time to be afraid right now. She needed to make them all see that, but how could she? What could she possibly say to make them follow her? She wasn't cut out for any of this. She'd been in their lives for all of five minutes, and now they were somehow expected to follow her lead? If she was in their place, she'd question her judgment, too. Out of the corner of her eye she could see Liam start to move towards her, ready to defend her, but she waved her hand, letting him know to stay put. She could do this.

"Keeping the sword safe is exactly what I'm trying to do here. But I can't do it alone. I may be an Aether-Born but that does not mean that I am indestructible.

There is still so much about my background that we don't know, but trust me when I tell you this, if there are other AetherBorns out there, ones that want to hurt everything we're trying to build here, they will pay for their actions. My loyalty is with you. My family."

She closed her eyes, reaching deep inside herself. She could sense the energy in the room shift, they were calmer now. She could still feel some fear in the room but that was unavoidable. "Look, I know you're scared." She looked around the room as she said it, trying to make eye contact with as many people as she could. "You should be. I'm scared, too. But we won't let them get us. Look at us! We've got four houses working together for the first time in centuries. We're freaking amazing!" her voice rose, and as it did, a light cheer went through the crowd. It was enough to make her relax.

"We'll start training tomorrow. The elders will divide you into groups and you'll be paired off with other Elementals that are more skilled in defence and battle." Liam jumped up next to her, "Everyone is expected to participate, so let's make sure we all find time each day to train."

Ruby looked around the room at the faces of the Elementals she was tasked with protecting. Some were smiling and eager but others still looked unsure. She didn't expect them to be following her into some battle. Whatever was coming for them next, she needed to make sure it stayed as far away from the center as possible. But that's not what mattered today. Today she needed to get them ready in case she wasn't around to shield them. In case she wasn't as strong as they all hoped she was. Watching them now, talking to each other eagerly, kids running around the room pretending to fight each other, she could breathe a sigh of relief.

They're going to be okay.

CHAPTER 33
HE WAS ALREADY MOVING ON

They walked back to her apartment in silence. After the meeting, she made sure to stick around for a bit to answer any questions people might have and to check in with her parents. Surprisingly, they were more relaxed than anyone else in the center. If she didn't know better, she'd think they even enjoyed being there to see the world their daughter was now a part of. The world she was expected to rule.

She had hoped Liam's parents would have preferred to stay in their quarters, but it seemed that they couldn't be happier to have an AetherBorn in power. It was all they could talk about when she finally got around to introducing them to her parents. She was certain that if Sebastian said the word 'tradition' one more time, her dad would blow a fuse. Liam had finally managed to get them away from each other, giving her a chance to talk to her parents alone.

They had a million questions and she tried her best to answer each one honestly. There was no point keeping them in the dark, especially if she needed them to stay alert in case any danger came their way. She told them about Ray and the dark liquid that had oozed from her eyes, making sure to leave out the part where she was attacked mid-sleep in her apartment. Knowing her parents, they'd be running around the room looking for volunteers to guard her bedroom at night.

"You have to promise me that if anything weird happens you'll come straight here, no questions asked." She said, when they refused her offer to move them into the center, "Even if you think it's stupid."

They had promised that much at least, and it should have been a relief to her, but walking back home now she still felt uneasy. Like she should have put her foot down and made them pack an overnight bag. At some point, she'd have to trust them to make their own decision about all of this. They were the parents after all.

"You think Shaylah's home?" Liam asked, as they climbed the stairs to her place.

"I don't think so. She said she had some date or something." Ruby couldn't help but smile, her friend just couldn't get enough of dating lately.

Ruby paused when she reached for the door handle, she could swear there were voices coming from inside the apartment. She put her finger to her lips, instructing Liam to be quiet. If she could barge in fast enough, she was sure she could get a good laugh for scaring Shaylah and a good laugh is exactly what she needed right now.

She pushed the door open and ran into the living room.

"Honey! I'm hom..." she yelled, but her words froze in mid-air.

She watched as Shaylah jumped back on the couch, struggling to cover herself with her shirt. Her hair, pulled back to one side, exposed the tattoo on her neck, and her face was red with embarrassment. Behind her, Jake's face stared at them, eyes wide with shock. He started buttoning up his own shirt, but Ruby was already walking past them into her room. Dragging an open-mouthed Liam behind her.

"Fish! Hang on!" Shaylah chased after her, "It's not what it looks like!"

But it was too late. Ruby had already seen more of their night than she wanted to. She pushed her hand to the door, black fog emerging from her palms, knocking the door shut before her friend could get closer. "It's not a big deal. Really. We'll talk later. You guys..." she paused, "Finish hanging out. Sorry we interrupted!"

She was sure that her friend felt terrible. And Jake? She had no idea what he might have felt. This is the same guy who just professed his love to her, then started acting like a complete moron when she didn't return his feelings. I guess it couldn't have meant all that much if he was already moving on. By hooking up with her best friend, no less.

What were they thinking? Had she really meant that little to them?

She was fuming. Ready to tear down the walls and level out the entire building, but something stopped her. Liam's hand pressed against her waist. The warmth and strength of it pulled her back into herself. Making her remember what home truly felt like. She let him pick her up and carry her to the bed.

Lying there, her head on his chest, rising and falling with each one of his breaths, she let herself cry the tears that had been refusing to come for days.

CHAPTER 34
SUCH A YOUNG GIRL

They sat on the training room floor in silence while Ruby tried to catch her breath. Her head was not in training today and Liam had managed to knock her on her butt a few times, already. The last fireball he sent towards her missed her by less than an inch. If she hadn't moved out of the way in time, she could have gotten seriously hurt.

Goddamnit! She thought, and pushed her head back to rest on the wall behind her. She was supposed to be looking for new AetherBorn powers, not screwing up her grip on the ones she already had.

She watched as Liam got up to grab a bottle of water from the table and handed it to her. Usually, she'd be able to knock him out with no problem during training, but this time around, he didn't so much as break a sweat while she was a hollow mess on the floor. "You all right today?"

Ruby thought about his question. She wasn't all right at all. "I don't know. Not really, I guess."

"Wanna talk about it?" He walked over and sat down next to her.

"I just don't get it."

"Jake and Shaylah?"

"Yeah. I had no idea they even liked each other. Why wouldn't they tell me?"

"Would that have made any difference?"

Her eyes studied his face in detail, trying to see if he was even remotely upset about her reaction to finding them together. She didn't want to hurt his feelings or make him question if she still had feelings for Jake, but she couldn't just shut off her surprise and hurt. He was asking her questions about it, so he couldn't be too bothered by it all. "Probably not." She said, "It's not that I even think I have any say in this. They're both adults, they can do what they want. It's just..."

"What?"

"Well, I thought we were all friends. Close friends. If they had the hots for each other they should have told me." She didn't add that Shaylah should have been the first one to let her know, since she knew how much Ruby used to care for Jake. She felt cheated and wronged. Like her friendships weren't what she thought they were.

"You sure that's all it is?" Liam could always tell when she was worried or upset. And in times like this, she hated that about him.

"I don't want you to think that I'm upset about Jake. I'm really not. It's just that Shay and I tell each other everything. I would've thought she would tell me if she started crushing on Jake. Especially since..." she stopped talking before she completely obliterated his feelings.

"You mean since you used to be into him for so long?"

"Uhm..."

"It's fine, Rue. I know you had a life before me. I can handle it."

"I don't even know if that's it. Maybe with everything that's going on, I just needed one thing in my life to not be confusing and a total mess. Whatever crap was going on with me and Jake, Shay was the one thing that was still normal. Now, I don't even know what I'm supposed to think."

Liam reached over and pulled her closer to him, his one hand brushing her cheek lightly. She let her head drop on his shoulder and nestled into the base of his neck, her body relaxing at his touch. At least this was one thing that was still the same. "I guess I shouldn't overthink it, though." She said quietly, "We have other things to worry about right now."

"Like what?"

"Dinner with your parents tonight, for starters." She looked up at him and forced a smile to her lips.

"Oh, yeah! That should be..." he paused, "Interesting."

Ruby looked away nervously. Lately, for her, interesting had a funny way of turning into catastrophic.

"So, Ruby, Liam tells me that you've made quite the progress at the center? It must be tough having everyone under one roof. I don't imagine the houses are too keen on getting along?"

"It's been pretty good, actually. I think we all expected a lot more push back when Ruby agreed to lead the houses." Liam said. He squeezed Ruby's hand under the table which made her nerves calm down.

"And how do *you* feel about it, Ruby?" Abigail gave her son a pointed look. Ruby did her best to stifle a laugh, she liked that his mom wanted to hear her opinion. She particularly liked that Liam had another woman in his life who was strong enough not to dote on his every word.

"I think it hasn't been as easy as everyone thinks it has been."

"How do you mean?" Sebastian raised one of his bushy eyebrows, "Are you having trouble with the Elementals?"

"No, not at all. I think I'm mostly having trouble accepting that I'm responsible for so many lives now." She was surprised the words left her mouth, but it was nice to have finally said it out loud. "Everyone keeps asking me what to do, and I don't want to say something that will upset anyone."

"I couldn't imagine having to be in charge of so many people, at your young age."

"Dad! Ruby's doing a great job leading us. We just need to trust that she knows what she's doing."

"I didn't mean any offence, Ruby. I only meant that you were thrown into this large role, it must be difficult to handle sometimes."

"It is. But it helps having all the house elders to turn to. They've been very supportive of my decisions, and it's nice to know that we're all working as a team."

"So, you still think it was the right decision—to divide the sword?" Abigail said. Ruby had almost forgotten that they didn't like changes being made to the traditional Elemental ways. "Even after some have already been stolen?"

"I really do." She needed to make them understand that she wasn't just some kid, "If my AetherBorn powers hadn't kicked in, it would have been catastrophic."

She remembered the vision of the future she had. The destruction caused by the Elementals in their pointless war for the sword. All of the deaths it brought. Her hand moved under the table and found Liam's. She was so happy he was here with her, that he believed in her vision for the future. No matter what his parents thought, she knew she'd made the right decision to take control away from Air and Water. She'd seen first-hand what would happen if she hadn't. "Besides," she said, "if the sword was still whole, whoever took the pieces would have the entire thing right now, and who knows what they plan on doing with it."

"True. Still, it seems like a lot of power to carry for such a young girl. Aren't you even a little afraid of the wrath? I certainly would be." Sebastian said. She hated his tone of voice. What did he know about the power she had?

"Well, the first AetherBorn was younger than I am when she was created, and by my age she managed to not only lead the Elementals but even have a child and hide her away from the elders." Her voice started to rise, "You'd be surprised what an AetherBorn can do when she puts her mind to it. And what wrath?"

"Oh, child. I forget how new you are to our world." His eyes held hers in an intensity she didn't much care for, "The wrath of the deities of course."

"Dad!" Liam yelped, "Stop filling her head with nonsense!"

"You mean the original Gods?" she asked, her interest fully peaked.

Sebastian toggled the words in his mouth, tasting them one by one before letting them roll off his tongue.

"Yes, my dear. They don't exactly like their ways to be meddled with. Especially not by someone who has been ignorant to our culture for most of her life."

"Ignorant to your culture?" Ruby lifted off her chair slightly, her voice was rising and she was furious. She felt the pressure of Liam's palm on her thigh under the table but not even he could stop her rage. "If it wasn't for me, you wouldn't have a culture to cling to right now! Remind me again where your precious deities were when the lot of you were about to slaughter each other into extinction? Because I don't remember anyone stepping forward to stop you except some *ignorant* child that somehow managed to settle down a war!"

Their skepticism should have wounded her. It should have amplified her doubts about herself and her ability as a leader. After all, that's what they intended to do tonight it seemed. But it did quite the opposite, it made her stronger somehow; forcing her to fight for her opinions and what she thought was right. They had no right to question her actions, not when they've been hiding away across the world while their son was trying to right the wrongs of their entire history without any help. With Liam's hand still holding unto her leg, she knew she had at least one supporter at the table, and that made her confident in her decisions.

She could see his parents were surprised at her outburst. Their faces were paler than they had been at the start of dinner, and they played uncomfortably with their silverware. They were still looking for a way to change the subject when Liam's phone rang. He excused himself and walked out of the dining hall towards the bathroom, only to reappear a minute later.

"We need to go." There was panic in his eyes that made her immediately worried, "Now."

Ruby got up from her seat without hesitation. If he was concerned, it had to be something big. She picked up her purse and excused herself from the table, following him to the exit. "Liam! Wait up! What happened?"

"That was Elena. The Air piece is gone."

CHAPTER 35
MY WELL-GUARDED HOME

There was a car waiting for them outside the restaurant. Elena must have sent one of her drivers to pick them up as soon as she realized the sword piece was stolen. Ruby felt uncomfortable that the mayor knew exactly where they would be tonight. The idea that she was a figure of authority now and her life was no longer her own had not sunk in until now. Was she no longer entitled to privacy? She didn't remember signing up for that.

Ruby tried to push the thought out of her mind. After all, there were more important things to worry about right now. Like another missing sword piece and who took it. It couldn't have been Ray this time; her cold body was stored in the medical lab in the center. So, who could be behind this?

As the car twisted and turned down familiar city

streets, her thoughts jumped between the theft and her own life. She looked over at Liam who seemed to be drowning in his own questions, much like she was. They made a sharp right turn and she slid across the back seat closer to him. His arm instinctively wrapped around her, pulling her into safety. As she settled into his chest, she couldn't help but think of their future together. Would there come a time when she'd be forced to choose between him and her role as an AetherBorn?

"Ruby! I'm so glad you came so fast!" Elena rushed over to them as soon as her bodyguards led them into the living room of her home.

This was the first time they'd visited the mayor in her house, and as the made their way through, Ruby's jaw was open wide enough that she thought it might dislocate. This was by far the most extravagant house she'd ever set foot in. The outside of the colonial home looked unremarkable. It was definitely large, with a small pond and circular driveway at the entrance, but it was the interior of the house that really packed a punch.

When the front door opened, Ruby expected to see a sitting room or a small hallway that would be reminiscent of the home's era. What she saw was something entirely different. The interior of the home had been gutted completely to make room for a ballroom sized entrance hall with a large, glass staircase leading to the sleeping quarters upstairs. There was an oversized barn door to their left which Ruby assumed led to the kitchen and dining area. To their right was an open-concept entrance to the living room where they now stood with Elena. The entire house was minimal, modern, and undeniably chic. Elena had definitely outdone herself.

"Of course." She said, and followed the mayor to one of the three couches that sat around a marble fire-place, "We came as soon as you called Liam. Thank you for the ride, by the way."

"It's the least I could do. Besides, I needed you here as soon as I realized what happened."

"What exactly do you think happened?" Liam asked, a pointed gaze on one of the bodyguards, "I thought you had eyes in and out of the safe room."

"We did. The guards were switching shifts. And before you start your antics, Liam, I already had them questioned. The room was only empty for a few minutes."

"Ray's room was only empty for a half hour and someone managed to kill her. We have to assume that whoever is behind this can get in and out of spaces pretty quickly."

"About that," Elena looked at Ruby, "we had cameras installed in the room after Cyril's piece went stolen."

Of course! Ruby thought. *Why the hell didn't we put those in every room?*

"But the footage is useless." Elena remarked, as if reading her mind, "This is all we can see."

She pushed the screen of her phone to Ruby. The image of the safe room appeared on an app with a timer running at the bottom. Ruby studied the room to see if anything looked out of place when the entire screen filled with black. Every detail covered with darkness and the only things still visible were the bright timer numbers on the bottom of the screen. After a few minutes, the fog disappeared, leaving the room in the same condition it was in before. They watched the footage until the room door opened and the next guard walked in to take his place as watch.

"Black fog." Ruby whispered.

"You're thinking it's an AetherBorn?"

"What else would it be, Liam? Nothing else that we know of can cover a room with that much darkness."

Elena paced the room. Her terracotta face was looking especially pale this evening. Ruby could tell she was upset about what happened, but it was more than just the sword piece. Something else was bothering her. "Elena, what's going on?"

"Other than someone coming into my home and taking something that belongs to me, you mean?"

"Well, yes. Is that all that's bothering you?"

"Is that all, Ruby? Is that all?" She lifted her hands

in the air as if to protest the question, "Someone came into my well-guarded home, broke into a room that was more secure than a bank safe, and somehow managed to do all of this undetected. They were in the house where I live, Ruby! With my children!"

Ruby was shocked at her reaction. She watched the tears stream down her cheeks, not knowing what to do next. Her initial instinct was to rush over to her and scoop her up into a hug but she knew Elena would not respond well to being touched. She glanced over at Liam who shook his head to tell her he was just as dumbfounded. "Elena, please, we can get you more security and we will find out who took the piece."

"You don't understand. What if Mihaela and Ioana had been home? What if they got in the way? What would any security do then?"

Ruby blinked her eyes rapidly, finally understanding. Elena couldn't care less about the sword piece. All she cared about were her children. She wasn't used to seeing any maternal emotion from the mayor but now that she understood why she was so upset, she felt closer to her. Like she was finally able to see through her guarded facade. She walked over, reaching for Elena's hands and holding them in hers. Their eyes met and she held her gaze for a few seconds before she started to speak. "The girls are safe, Elena. I promise you that. I will die before I let anything happen to them." From the corner of her eye she could see Liam wince at the mention of her dying, but she blew right past it, "If it will make you feel safer, you can all come stay at the center until you feel more comfortable coming home."

"Even the guards?" Elena smiled, and pointed at the suited men at the door.

"Even the guards," she said, and sat back down. "Liam, can you do me a favor?"

"Sure, what?"

"Call an elder meeting. I think we're all feeling out of our element right now. I might know how to put everyone's mind at ease for the time being."

"For the time being?" Elena raised a questioning eyebrow.

Ruby's hand reached for hers and squeezed it reassuringly. "Until we catch the bastard that's doing this, and end it once and for all."

CHAPTER 36
A QUEEN SHOULD HAVE A KNIGHTHOOD

The air in the library was filled with disappointment and fear. Ruby leaned on one of the book shelves and tried to read each elder's expression, but could not figure out if they were upset about the latest break in, or eager to hear why they were called in for an emergency meeting. Cyril was the hardest to read, brooding at the edge of his seat and avoiding eye contact with everyone in the room. If Ruby didn't know better, she'd think he was responsible for the theft. Unfortunately, the mystery was not so easy to solve. All she knew was that an AetherBorn broke into Elena's home and was in and out within minutes.

But how did they use the fog to get into the room? Ruby had been trying to manipulate it for weeks and had not been able to even get close to teleportation.

A. N. SAGE

"Thanks for coming here so quickly." She moved closer to the table to address the room, "I'm sure you're wondering why I asked for this meeting."

"We're assuming it's about the latest theft?" Cyril finally looked up from his lap, his sharp eyes digging into her very soul.

"Sort of. I mean, yes. Kind of," she realized how foolish she sounded, but kept going. "We still aren't any closer to finding who's responsible. And with only one sword piece left, we're running out of time."

"But we've done everything we can! We secured all the pieces. There're guards on every door for God's sake!" Myriam exclaimed. "What else can we be doing?"

"That's the thing though," she sat down and leaned into them, her voice almost a whisper. "Every time we do something, whoever is stealing the pieces is one step ahead. It's like they know what we're going to do next before we even do it."

"Are you suggesting there's a spy amongst the Elementals?" Alice's eyes widened, and she looked around the room like she was trying to spot the traitor.

"It's the only thing that makes sense." She thought back to the greenhouse and the eyes she felt on her and Liam. "Whoever this AetherBorn thief is, they're being fed information. They knew where the pieces are kept, they knew when they'd be less watched, they even knew

180

when the guards changed spots! I don't think there's any other way for them to have known all this unless someone was telling them everything we said in here."

"But why? Who would do that?" Liam interrupted, confused like the rest of them. She had told him before they started the meeting not to draw attention to himself. Cyril and Elena were still not comfortable with someone who was not an elder being a part of these meetings, but they made an exception out of respect for Ruby. Of course, he couldn't help but offer his opinion every chance he got, which made her blood boil with anger. "What would they have to gain?"

"I'm not sure." She shot a pointed look in his direction and he immediately sat back down, "The point is that we have to be careful who we trust right now."

"There are hundreds of Elementals coming through here every day. We'll have to sew our lips shut and stay in our quarters if we want to contain everything." Elena threw her hands up, slapping them on her lap in frustration.

"You don't have quarters here," Cyril smiled.

"Actually, as of last night, I do. Maybe you should, too, until we figure out who's behind all this."

Ruby sat up straight in her chair and played with the frayed edges of the book next to her. Elena had a point. With all of them under one roof it would be easier for her to rule them out as suspects. It's not that she didn't trust the elders, but something was definitely off about the entire situation. "That's not a bad idea, Elena. It'll be good to have everyone here in case we need them. I actually had another idea, too."

"What kind of idea?" Liam asked. His brow scrunched and she knew he was already worried about her. He had every right to be, her ideas usually put her straight in the line of fire.

"Well, so far we've been on the defensive. A piece gets stolen and we put up more guards. Another gets stolen and we train everyone to fight. What if we could get ahead of it? Bring the thief to us instead?"

"Like a trap?"

"Yes, exactly like a trap."

"What did you have in mind, Ruby?" Cyril asked.

"We make them think something big is going to happen. Deflect them from the remaining sword piece while we move it. Basically, I want to trick the mole."

"Give them wrong information so they pass it on to the AetherBorn..."

"Exactly. But we'll have to make it convincing. They won't bite unless they think we have some big plan."

"And how do we do that?"

"I was thinking we use me as bait."

Liam got up, his fists hitting the table with a bang. His green eyes were wild with fury and she could have sworn she saw his hands start to steam, fire forming on his fingertips. "Hell no! You're not playing bait again!"

"Liam, please calm down. It's not going to be like last time." She said, looking over at Cyril and Elena and hoping they didn't mind her bringing up what happened before the treaty. "I'm thinking we just make whoever is spying on us believe that we have some big plan about to happen. We use me as a distraction. Then, when they fall for the whole thing, we plan a time for the fake event to happen and wait until the AetherBorn comes to us."

"And how exactly are we going to convince them that you have some big event planned?"

"Put more security on me. Have them follow me around day and night, like I'm, all of a sudden, top priority."

"You're always top priority," Liam said. "You're basically our queen."

"Well, a queen should have a knight's guard, no?" She smiled. She kind of liked the idea of having her own knights. "If the spy thinks I'm guarding something important, they'll for sure pass that information on. Playing right into our hands."

"You don't think they'll find it odd that a bunch of Elementals are crowding you, all of a sudden?"

Liam had a point. She'd never had security before, in fact, she mostly argued against the idea. They would need to work hard to convince the spy that her personality could have changed over-night. "So, let's make it real. Let's train the 'knights' here in the center. Actually train them. We're strengthening everyone's powers so it shouldn't be too strange that we're training a fighting force. We'll try to keep it as secret as possible but make sure to throw hints in conversations. We want this to be believable. If there was some secret mission and I was putting together an entire personal army, I wouldn't go around advertising it to everyone."

"It could work." Alice spoke for the first time today, "It won't be easy, but it could work."

"And if it doesn't?" Liam asked.

"Then at least I'll have my 'knights' to protect me." She could see he liked that answer.

"I'm going to be on this team. No arguments."

Her face brightened. She wasn't going to argue with him, when she came up with the idea, she already knew who she wanted in her knighthood and Liam was the first person she had in mind. She wouldn't dare trust her safety to anyone else, even if it was all fake. "I figured as much. So yes, of course you will be. Jake, too, he's one of our strongest Water fighters. And we'll need a few more volunteers. Some from each house. We'll need all the powers activated if we have any trouble with the thief."

"This is starting to feel like the competition for the sword our ancestors had." Cyril noted.

"Except no one is fighting to the death this time."

THEY WALKED BACK to Liam's room quietly. There was a lot to be done in the next few days. They'd have to round up the recruits and get their training started. Ruby would have to figure out where to move the remaining sword pieces to, and secretly make a copy of the Onyx necklace. She never took it off and it would be too suspicious if it was gone now. Besides, if the thief wanted to steal the piece, they'd have to come after her, which would only strengthen her plan.

She was starting to get worried. If it didn't work exactly as she planned, she could be in real danger and so could everyone around her. Pulling Liam and Jake into the knighthood only put them in harm's way. Failing at this was not an option. She needed to be prepared for an actual attack, which meant her powers had to be in full control. Her own training was just as important as the knights. She couldn't afford to let her personal life get in her head which only meant one thing. All of her relationships and their drama were on hold until this was finished. A sadness washed over her face. *Even Liam.*

"You think this'll actually work?" he asked, as if hearing his name in her head.

She tightened her fingers around his shirt and pulled him towards her. Raising herself up to her toes, she let her lips linger next to his, breathing in the hot air escaping them. Her hands travelled under his shirt and up his muscular back, tracing every curve while she pulled him in closer. Her lips pressed to his, devouring him. She tried to stay in that moment, remembering the taste of his mouth, how his tongue felt on hers. Her legs trembled as she pulled away, ready for whatever came next.

"It had better work," she said, "or we're screwed."

CHAPTER 37
EVERYONE WORKING TOGETHER

The elder's selection of fighters was better than Ruby had expected. They had somehow managed to find twelve of the strongest Elementals in the center without drawing too much attention to the proceedings. There were still a lot of skills they needed to perfect, but even the Earth fighters showed strength in the trainings. Some were even strong enough to shift the ground beneath their opponent's feet without needing to use a lot of their energy. As each training session came to an end, Ruby got a little more hope that if there was an attack coming their way, they would have a fighting chance to beat it. She remembered a time not long ago when the houses were still fighting each other, and was relieved to see everyone working together.

They used the training sessions to find ways for the

houses to combine their strengths. Air Elementals practiced on directing winds at fires Liam and his team created, making the bursts of flame spread faster. They even figured out how to use the power the Water house had to manipulate weather patterns as a means of creating shields. Ruby made sure that in each training they practiced lines of defence as well as attack. There was so much they didn't know about the AetherBorn behind the thefts, and she wanted to be ready for anything that might come their way.

Despite the fact that the knighthood was formed under pretenses to divert the spy in the center, by the end of the week it had started to feel as though it was very much real.

Ruby's own powers got stronger as she spent more of her time practicing. She realized that the more she connected to the Onyx stone, the more power she was able to borrow from the sword. As the days progressed, her visions started appearing on command, allowing her an advantage in battle. She wasn't able to see very far into the future but just enough to read her opponents next move before they made it. A useful trick to have on hand, but one that drained her of energy very quickly.

Training alongside the other houses also gave her the opportunity to see how they harnessed their abilities, and after a few days of trying, she was able to switch between AetherBorn and Elemental powers effortlessly. Her favorite move was to shield herself completely by surrounding her body in black fog; giving her a chance to surprise her opponent with an Elemental attack. The first time she did this, she catapulted Jake and two other Water knights across the room with gusts of wind while they were still trying to figure out what she was up to. Ruby couldn't help but smile as Jake dusted himself off, feeling like she had somewhat leveled the playing field for what happened with Shaylah.

Their training today was one of the longest ones they'd had so far. Ruby was hunched over a table and gulping down water breathlessly. She had just finished attacking five knights to test their defenses and was completely drained. She needed to stop harnessing the power of the Onyx for a few days or she would be completely worn out and useless if something did happen.

Her gaze circled Liam, tracing every curve of his muscles as he practiced an attack. They'd barely had a minute alone since the knighthood was formed. Ruby knew that she was the one who stayed away from him in order to concentrate on the training, but she couldn't help but miss him. She wondered if he noticed her absence, too, or if he was too entranced in practice to remember that they hadn't seen each other privately in almost a week. Liam was taking the knighthood even more seriously than she was, training until the late hours of the night and barely taking breaks. She took comfort in the fact that at least they were both equally committed to the plan.

As he started to charge forward, she saw the ruby ring on his finger light up. The brighter it shone, the stronger his hits were. She watched the ring glow as hot as the sun itself when Liam shot his last fireball.

The stones! She thought, and ran to him.

"Liam! I've got it!" she yelled.

He turned to her, breathing laboriously. His eyes squinted as he tried to understand what she was trying to say. "Got what?"

"The stones, we need to get stones for everyone! The bigger the better!" She pulled him excitedly towards the door, "We need to find Alice!"

CHAPTER 38

NOT THERE ANYMORE

"That's brilliant, Rue! If we can get enough stones, we'll amplify all their powers, by who knows how much." Liam trailed behind her, understanding what she was so excited about.

"I can't believe we hadn't thought of it before. Some of the fighters are already using them but we need to get stones to everyone in the center. It'll at least give them a better chance to protect themselves in case something happens."

"Yeah. Good call tapping Alice in, she's been feeling out of the loop lately."

"Plus, she's like a walking encyclopedia when it comes to Elementals. She's our best bet at getting the information out to everyone in the center."

As they approached Alice's quarters, Ruby felt a knot form in her stomach. Her vision started to blur. She wiped the sweat forming on her top lip and shot a concerned look in Liam's direction. His face immediately betrayed any facade of calm he could have mustered in the moment. He had learned very quickly that Ruby's gut instincts were nothing to toy with.

They started to knock when a loud bang came from inside the room. Liam pushed open the door without hesitation and they barged in, hands up and ready for attack.

The sitting area in Alice's quarters was silent and undisturbed. They slowly walked forward, trying to keep their movements minimal and undetected. Ruby nudged Liam's arm and pointed at the black shoe prints on the white carpet. Someone had definitely been here, Alice would never let this mess into her rooms. There were whispers coming from the bedroom and they made their way towards the sound.

The door of Alice's bedroom was slightly ajar, not enough for them to see anything but enough to hear what was going on inside.

"You should have done as I said." A harsh voice growled from the room.

Ruby could see Liam's face turn white. Something was wrong. She could feel it. Her hand pushed open the door and they ran inside.

As they entered the bedroom, Ruby's stomach turned. She clutched one hand at the doorway, trying to steady herself. Out of the corner of her eye she could see

Liam's hand burn, getting ready to throw fire. But her attention wasn't on him. Her eyes faced forward, looking towards the bed and Alice's unmoving body. Black, acidic molasses was eating through her flesh. Ruby watched in horror as a fireball shot past her, hitting the chest of the AetherBorn standing over Alice. She blinked her eyes to make sure she was seeing things correctly. It couldn't be real. The AetherBorn in front of them was...

"How is it a guy?" Liam yelled, readying his hands for another attack. The first didn't seem to make a difference, the tall man in front of them wasn't so much as phased by the hit. "We need to get to Alice!"

He ran towards the bed, putting up a wall of fire between himself and the AetherBorn.

"Liam! Don't touch her!" Ruby screamed, remembering the burns she got from touching Ray's face. She wanted to run to him, to help him get Alice off the bed but her eyes were still on the AetherBorn. He was so still that for a second, she thought he was frozen in time. That was, until he looked up with an evil grin on his face and eyes full of black. She wanted to slap the smile right off him but all she could do was stare at his eyes; they were the same as she remembered hers being in the vision.

"Hello, Ruby. It's about time we met. The name is Demas." He said, so softly it was almost a whisper. "I was wondering when I was finally going to be able to see you for myself." He took a step back, resting his lanky body on the backs of one of the chairs. His sharp nose pointed towards her like an AetherBorn divining rod. He tucked something into the pocket of his long leather coat. *The Fire piece.*

"Who the hell are you?" she yelled, charging towards him.

"I'm someone you shouldn't mess with."

Ruby's hands moved fast, surrounding herself in black fog, she was almost right next to him when she felt a hand reach through her barrier, squeezing her arm so hard that her bones felt as if they were turning to dust. She yelled out in pain and tried to yank her arm back but before she could get away, he caught her other arm in a death-grip. She was struggling to fight him off, squirming and trying to tap into her powers but nothing worked.

"Rue!" Liam's voice echoed behind her, his footsteps getting closer.

She could hear him scream for her but it was getting farther and farther away. As though the sound in the room was disappearing. Demas's hands held her tighter and she could see black veins start to trickle up her arm where he touched her.

What is this guy? She thought and tried to push him away unsuccessfully. She kicked at his shins, hoping to get some reaction that would give her enough time to free herself from his grip. He was unmoving. His stare burned into her, and he scowled as more tears fell down her cheeks.

Another fireball hit next to them; Liam was not going to stop.

"He's going to kill you if you don't let me go!" she shouted.

Demas's grin widened. The black in his eyes slowly dissipated, allowing for the warm brown of his irises to come through. His hands loosened and he took a step backward, his gaze never leaving Ruby's. "It doesn't matter. We're already there."

"Already where?"

Ruby looked down at her arms, the black veins receded and disappeared as though they were never there. She looked back at Demas, trying to figure out what was going on, when her gaze caught something bright to her left. She looked over, her mouth dropping to her chin.

Liam's fireball was suspended in mid-air, unmoving.

Her eyes followed the path of the fire back to Liam. His hands outstretched and mid attack. He was as frozen as his fire. As she looked around the room, she realized everything was standing still and she was the only one moving.

"What the hell did you do?" she demanded.

"Oh, Ruby. You still have so much to learn." Demas started to walk towards her but she backed away, "I didn't do anything at all."

"Then why is everything frozen? Why is Liam like that?"

"It isn't frozen where *he* is. We're just not there anymore."

She couldn't stand the sound of his voice. The growls that formed at the end of each sentence. She wanted to hurt him. To kill him. She didn't know if Alice was all right, but whatever this guy did to her, he would pay. "Where are we, then?" She asked, trying to keep him talking while her hands worked to power herself up. She put her palms together, turning them to point at Demas. Nothing happened. She tried again, waiting for the blast of wind to propel towards him but her Water powers were completely turned off somehow.

"Don't waste your time, darling." He laughed, tossing ringlets of black hair around his face. "Elemental powers are useless in the Aether Plane."

CHAPTER 39

THE SPARKLE IN THE AIR

The air around them glittered with the brilliance of perfectly cut diamonds. It was thicker than the normal air she was used to, like it was coating the entire room in some sort of barrier. Ruby ran towards Liam who was still completely motionless. As she ran, her feet kicked apart the black fog that floated close to the floor and Ruby felt a little like a child kicking puddles in the rain.

Her hand reached towards Liam but when she went to shake him to wake him up from whatever trance he was in, she tumbled forward. Her arm moved right through his body, causing it to turn into a fog, and to reassemble back into his figure immediately. She swatted at him again without making contact. Her eyes turned to Demas who seemed to be enjoying himself watching her.

"The Aether Plane?" Ruby asked, "What's happening to Liam? Why can't I touch him?"

"Forgive me, I forget that you know nothing of who you are. Think of this place as another way of existing. Somewhere only AetherBorns can go. Kind of like dreaming except you're very much awake." A sly smile formed at the corner of his thin lips, "I could teach you; you know? But you'll have to drop this whole charade you have with the Elementals. I'm sure the shadow of the crown is starting to wear its toll on you by now."

"It's not a charade. I don't know who you think you are, but you're not getting the sword. And I don't need you to teach me anything!" she roared.

Demas's hands made a quick motion across his chest and before Ruby could understand what happened, he pushed a black, plasma like substance towards her. As the ray of plasma shot towards her legs it started to shift. It moved fluidly, changing from a black liquid to something more solid. Ruby was amazed at what she was seeing and when she finally realized that she should get out of its way it was too late. The chain that the liquid turned into wrapped tightly against her leg. Demas pulled his arm back sharply, making the chain rip towards him, knocking Ruby straight on her butt. "You sure about that?"

How the hell did he do that? She trembled.

She tried to scramble back to her feet but before she could manage to get up, Demas shot another plasmic ray, this time aiming at her arm. The ray moved quicker than the last one as its tip sharpened before her eyes. As it reached her body, it was no longer a ray of plasma but a knife, slicing through her flesh with wicked speed. She yelled out at the burning pain pulsating through her shoulder. Her shirt was ripped where the knife had cut her, and black fluid oozed from the wound. She wiped at the wetness and got up. Not bothering to worry about the burns forming on her hand from touching the fluid.

Ruby wasn't about to give up that easily. If she couldn't use her Elemental powers here, maybe her AetherBorn abilities would still work. She concentrated on the Onyx around her neck, using her one good arm to push a black fog shot towards Demas's chest. To her surprise, instead of fog, her hand shot the same plasma he had used to attack her. Demas jumped out of the way fast enough to avoid it, throwing a look of confusion her way.

"Looks like I can teach myself just fine." She said, as confidently as she could, but inside she was shaking.

She got ready to attack again. Her hands moved in unison and she pushed through the pain in her arm to get a stronger connection to her powers. The Onyx glowed brighter, illuminating her collarbone in this dim darkness. She started to run towards Demas but before she could reach him, a sharp pain hit her thighs. She looked down to see the tip of a plasmic arrow protruding from her leg. The arrow started to turn back to liquid, burning the inside of her leg as it flowed down her thigh. The pain of it was excruciating. Ruby fell to the ground, holding onto her leg. She was just inches away from Liam, his face red with anger, still locked mid attack.

"Don't be stupid, Ruby. You have no idea what you're dealing with."

Demas walked towards her. A few more seconds and he would kill her, she had no doubt of that. This couldn't be how she died. In some Aether Plane she didn't even understand, cowering on the floor and licking her wounds. She couldn't let it end this way. She had to get back to Liam somehow. Her arm swatted through the glitter in the air, pushing it aside in slow tufts of smoke. She pushed her hand farther, reaching for Liam, picturing her holding him again. His thick arms pulling her close and tightening around her waist. This time as she wrapped her grip around his arm, it didn't fall right through. She could feel his skin in her hand. Hot and full of fire. The longer she held him, the more heat she gathered into herself until all the sparkle in the air around them turned to embers.

She shifted her gaze back to Demas, his eyes wide. He was no longer walking towards her but was standing still, watching the Aether Plane disappear.

Her leg was still throbbing and she wanted to put pressure on the wound but her hand would not let go of Liam. She closed her eyes, letting herself picture him next to her. Her energy was draining fast and she felt sick but kept going. Her mind never leaving his side.

"Rue! Rue!" She heard him call out, "Can you hear me?"

Ruby opened her tear stained eyes and looked up at him. He was at her side now, using a piece of cloth he tore from his tee to wipe her legs. "What happened? How did you get this?"

She was so weak. Her eyes felt heavier than they had in days. She looked back at the spot where Demas was just standing, but there was nothing more than traces of black fog in the air. She tried to sit up, but her body collapsed into Liam's chest. She fought the losing battle of sleep taking her over.

She moved her gaze to the bed. The sight of Alice's limp, ooze-covered body was the last thing she remembered before the world went dark.

CHAPTER 40
FLASHES OF DISCOMFORT

"Take it easy." Liam hovered over her when she finally opened her eyes.

She had no recollection of the last twenty-four hours, with the exception of falling in and out of sleep. Her head was throbbing, and invisible mallets punched her temples in repeating patterns. When she tried to sit up, a stabbing pain shot up the side of her leg, immediately reminding her of what happened. "How long was I out?"

"About a day. I thought I should let you rest so you could recover." He looked down at her leg. The cut itself seemed to have healed, but she could still feel the burning from the plasma and wondered how long it'd take for it to go away.

"Liam," she reached for his hand and sat up, "is

Alice..." She didn't know how to finish the sentence without crying.

Luckily, Liam sensed her pain and decided to jump in. "Yes," he said, and turned away. His face betrayed every hurt and ache he felt in the moment. She squeezed his hand, sending flashes of discomfort to her bruised arm. She couldn't even begin to imagine what he was going through.

"I'm so sorry. I swear, I'm going to kill this guy." Ruby pressed her fists into the bed. "He won't get away with this."

"I still don't even understand what happened. One second, you were standing next to me and the next you're just gone. I checked the entire room and nothing. Then you were back again but cut up, with an arrow in your leg and this guy was nowhere to be found. Who the hell was that?"

"Demas. He said his name is Demas. I think he's the AetherBorn we've been after."

"How is that possible? A dude?"

Ruby was just as surprised as he was. There had not been evidence of a male AetherBorn in any of the books they'd researched. As far as they could tell, only the females in the lineage received the sword call, which was why it skipped over her dad and went straight to her. "I have no clue. But I don't think he's alone. The way he kept talking, all confident, it was like he had more people working with him. Maybe even more AetherBorns."

"How many more?"

"No idea. But this guy is no joke. He knows how to do things that I've never seen or read about. I don't think anyone here has." She thought back to their encounter. "I was there you know. When you shot that last fireball, I was right there. It was the weirdest thing. I was right next to you but in a different place at the same time."

"Different place?"

"Yeah. Demas called it an Aether Plane. Some plane of existence where time was moving but everything outside is frozen in place, at least it was to me. It was so disorienting. Like I was there with you, but you were, like, a movie on a screen, paused or something like that." Her hand waved at her arm and leg. "How is that even possible?"

"I have no idea. You literally vanished. Just gone. Not for very long, just a few minutes really, but still... Gone."

"It didn't feel like a few minutes to me. I was there long enough for him to cause all this damage." Her hand gestured over her leg.

"Wait, but how? I didn't see any weapons on him and you look like you ran blind-folded through an armory."

"That's the weird thing. My Elemental powers don't

work there at all but my AetherBorn powers..." She paused, "They're different."

Liam leaned in closer, brushing a stray hair away from her eyes. "Different how?"

"I don't even know how to explain it. It's not a fog like it is here but something thick. Some sort of plasma. I think that's how Demas hurt me. It was like he was able to turn that plasma into actual weapons laced with its poison."

"That would explain why you had trouble healing. Your wound didn't close like your other ones did until I was able to get all that black soot out of it."

"You didn't touch it, right?"

"No. I learned my lesson after..." he stopped talking.

Alice. She thought when she saw the burn marks on his fingers. He probably tried to save her life.

"Liam, we'll get him." She said, knowing nothing she said right now could make it better.

"You might want to call your parents. Your phone was going off non-stop all day."

He wasn't ready to talk about Alice and she needed to respect that. As much as she wanted to hold him and intrude on his emotions, she knew better than to open a wound that wasn't yet healed. Her hands caught the cell phone he tossed her way. Twenty-seven missed calls. An unnecessary amount, even for her parents.

When she went through the list, she realized most of the calls were not from her family's number at all, they were Shaylah's. She tried to remember if they had plans that she might have missed but nothing came to mind. Either her friend wanted to talk about Jake or she was worried when Ruby didn't come home last night.

She couldn't keep lying to her. If Alice's death taught her anything, it's that no one in her life was safe, and now that Shaylah was also involved with Jake, there was a good chance she'd be in danger. Something about the way Demas looked at her before he vanished, it was a mix of hatred and admiration. She only saw one other person look at her that way before, and Cyril ended up killing someone she loved as a result. She wasn't going to risk Shaylah's life just to keep her secret. Her speech about preparing for the worst wasn't meant just for the Elementals. Everyone who touched her life needed protection.

Liam was watching her gather her thoughts. She would need to let him know what she was planning later, but all she could think of right now was the best way to protect her friend. The faster she could move her into the center, the better.

CHAPTER 41

HOW DO YOU FEEL ABOUT
BASEMENTS?

Shaylah burst into the coffee shop and giddily ran over to the table Ruby saved for them. She had already ordered a few coffees and was fumbling with the sugar spoon when her friend plonked down on the seat across from her. The table shook from the impact and Ruby tried to hold on to her cup to avoid a spill.

"I'm so glad you wanted to meet!" Shaylah bellowed, popping a sugar cube into her mouth. She had a very odd taste in snacks.

"Yeah, me, too. I guess there's a bit we need to talk about."

"Look, Fish, I seriously wasn't planning anything with Jake. I swear, girl. I figured you were totes over him by now, but it was stupid, and insensitive, and I'm sorry.

I won't see him again." Shaylah's eyes never left the coffee in front of her when she spoke.

Ruby reached over for her friend's hand. She still felt awkward about Jake and her, but that was the last of her worries right now. The thought of Shaylah getting hurt again put everything in perspective. Whatever feelings she had would need to be put on hold until Demas was no longer a threat. Ruby was starting to feel like her entire life had to be put on hold for this jerk. "Shay, it's not about Jake."

"Wait, what? I thought you'd be hella pissed at me."

"I'm not. I mean I was." She paused to think about her next words, "Not pissed, just surprised and a little hurt. I figured you'd have told me, that's all."

"Fish, I swear. It just kind of happened and I wanted to tell you, but you haven't been around forever. You're always with Liam now and it's been hard to get you alone to talk."

"Yeah, about that. That's actually why I wanted to meet today."

"About Liam? Is he okay? Are you okay? Did he hurt you? I'll freakin' kill him!"

"Oh my god, calm down," she laughed. "He's fine and I'm fine. But there's a reason that I've been spending so much of my time with him."

"Are you preggers?"

"Geez, Shay. No."

"Okay, so what is it?"

"Some stuff happened a little while ago that kind of put me in this new position that's taking up a lot of my time. I don't even know where to start."

"Just start anywhere. I'm dying to know what's going on!"

Ruby took a big gulp of her coffee. Whether she was ready for it or not, she was about to expose her friend to something that most people would find unbelievable. She was worried that she'd sound crazy, that her friend would walk away and write her off entirely, but her gut was gnawing at her to speak up. Somehow, she felt this would play out just fine. "Okay, but we need to go somewhere first." She said and motioned for her friend to follow her out. "How do you feel about basements?"

CHAPTER 42

FAVORITE PLACES

Shaylah's mouth didn't shut almost the entire tour through the center. She wanted to see and touch everything. Ruby was impressed with how her friend was taking the news. The first time Ruby mentioned the Elementals, she saw the confusion on Shaylah's face and almost stopped telling her but after explaining everything that'd happened, Shaylah seemed to be on board.

"Hey, so is every Elemental hot like Liam or did you just get lucky?" she winked as they made their way to the greenhouse. "Oh! And what powers do you have? You said there're powers! Can I see?"

Ruby couldn't help but laugh at all the questions. She wondered if she would be just as excited if she had gotten thrown into this world the way Ruby had, or had the responsibilities she now had. "I'll show you some cool stuff after. Come check this out!" Ruby pulled at her friend's furry jacket sleeve, dragging her into the greenhouse.

"Holy crap! This place is so gorge!" she screamed.

"It's one of my favorite places. Liam's too. We come here all the time to..."

"Make out?" Shaylah asked, giggling.

"To think. We come here all the time to think." Ruby was shaking her head but her memories of sneaking away here after training to spend time with Liam made her blush. "And sometimes to make out." She added and laughed.

"I freakin' knew it! So, what's it like getting into it with an Elemental?"

"Well, actually..." she started to speak but was interrupted by a cough at the door. They whipped their heads around to see Jake standing in the doorway, a disapproving look on his face. Shaylah's eyes darted from Jake to her, trying to piece the puzzle together until it finally made sense.

"No way!" She yelled, "You, too?"

"Ruby, can I speak with you outside for a second?" Jake asked completely ignoring Shaylah.

"Uhm, sure. Shay, I'll be right back, 'kay?"

She barely made it out the door when he was towering over her, his anger dripping from every word he spewed. "How can you bring her here? What were you thinking?" He shouted, balling his hands into fists.

"You need to lower your voice. Immediately." Her tone was cold and collected. Friend or not, she wasn't going to let anyone speak to her that way. "If you can't have a proper conversation right now, we can continue this when you've had a chance to calm down."

She turned around to walk away but he chased after her. "I'm sorry. I won't yell. Just please explain to me what she's doing here?"

"The same thing everyone is doing here, Jake. She's going to learn to defend herself."

"But why? Why would you tell her about us? She was safer before; this wasn't just your secret to tell!" His voice was starting to rise again.

"Was she safe when a bank fell on her, Jake? Or when my apartment was broken into? By your dad, might I add." She saw him start to look down and moved her body closer to him, forcing him to look her in the eyes. "Alice was an elder. The strongest one of her house, and she wasn't safe. You think a little human girl could protect herself against what's coming?"

He was quiet. Jake shifted his weight from leg to leg, swaying back and forth like a kid that needed to use the bathroom. She was his superior and he knew it but something was still bothering him. It was as if he didn't want Shaylah here even if it meant protecting her. "What exactly is coming then?"

"We don't know, yet," she lied, "but whatever it is, I'm not risking her life just to keep your secret. You need to figure it out and deal with it. I'm moving her into the center. It's the only way for me to make sure she's safe."

"So, just like that? I don't get a say?"

"No, Jake, I'm sorry. You don't."

He looked her up and down, the anger on his face changing into something else. She couldn't quite put her finger on it. It was a strange mixture of hurt and disgust which made her wonder how someone who was supposed to love you could look at you like they despised you at the same time. She wanted to tell him that she was sorry. To explain everything that'd happened with Demas, and to show him how scared she was but it was too late. By the time she started to speak, he was already walking away from her.

Ruby turned around and went back into the green-house, realizing that Jake was no longer hers. And by the way he just acted, she wasn't sure he was Shaylah's either.

"Where'd Jake go?"

"Oh. Uhm, he had a lesson to get to," she lied.

"Right."

Her friend's face looked sad, like she knew Ruby was lying but didn't want to find out the truth. She wondered how much Shaylah cared for Jake. How quickly she might have fallen for him. If anyone knew what it was like to pine after his affections, it was Ruby.

She placed her arm around Shaylah's shoulder and pulled her away from the door. Back into the safety of the greenhouse and away from the possibility of Jake's rejection. "Come on! I'll show something cool I can do with these plants!"

CHAPTER 43
DISCOVERING NEW TERRITORIES

They spent a few more hours in the center walking from room to room so Shaylah could get better acquainted with her new surroundings. She sure was getting a kick out of all the nooks in the center, asking to see each new room and rushing over to meet everyone. Ruby was expecting her to be more put off by the idea of spending time here indefinitely but Shaylah could not get home to pack her overnight bags faster. When Jake offered to accompany her that night, Ruby finally understood why she was so excited to move in. Turns out Shaylah's crush on Jake was a little more than just a simple infatuation. She felt foolish for not having seen it sooner. Was she really that preoccupied lately?

She considered going with them to get some more of her own things since she was getting pretty tired of wearing the same three sweatshirts and jeans on rotation but by the time the sun set, she was all out of steam. Her leg was still sore from the arrow wound and all she wanted was to lie down next to Liam and rest.

Her pulse raced faster the closer she got to his room. This would be the first time in a week that she would get to spend time alone with him and she couldn't make it to the room fast enough. She felt a flutter of air on the back of her neck and spun around to see who was there. The hallway was empty with the exception of two Air kids playing farther down. She was sure she felt someone right behind her, the pressure of not knowing who the spy is was starting to get to her. There was a hint of black fog in the air. She waved her hand around to disperse it, not even realizing that she had started to set off her powers in her state of fear.

You have got to get your head back on straight! She yelled at herself and continued to make her way to Liam's room. Not bothering to knock, she pushed the door open and rushed inside, locking her paranoia behind.

"Hey you!" He jumped up on his bed, clearly startled by her entrance. His hands felt around to find a shirt to put on but after a week away from him, she didn't mind the sight of his bare chest one bit.

"Wait 'til I tell you about today!" Ruby kicked off her shoes and threw her arms around him, pressing against every hard curve of his abdomen.

"I take it things went well with Shaylah?"

"Yep! She can't wait to get in here!" Her hand moved up and down his chest playfully. "There was some weirdness with Jake but it's fine now. He went to get her stuff with her so at least we know she'll be safe. If I could just get my parents in here!"

"You worry too much about everyone else, you know that?" Liam's hand cupped her chin and pushed it up so that his lips were right next to hers. He grazed her bottom lip lightly and she could feel the hairs on her neck rise from his touch. "Sometimes you need to do what's best for *you.*" He pulled her closer, his fingers wrapping themselves in her hair. Her body flooded with warmth under his weight. She stared into his eyes, craving to be kissed by him again. Wanting him on every inch of her.

"Ow!" Ruby suddenly jumped back, being all too aware of the pain in her thigh.

"What happened? Are you all right?"

"Yeah. Sorry. It's my leg, I think it's still..."

"Let me see it!" Before she could stop him, his hands reached for her jeans, pulling them off to inspect her wound. There was no visible cut but it was a throbbing red that was painful to look at. "Does it hurt when I touch it?" He asked and pushed two fingers into her leg.

"No. Try again." She watched as he pushed her thigh with his hand, squeezing it gently but with some force. When he realized she was just toying with him, he reached up to pinch her arm which made her laugh even more.

"Rue! I was actually worried!"

"I'm fine. Please stop worrying. It's just a little pain now and then, it'll go away soon."

His eyes met hers and she could see there was something he wanted to say but couldn't. She placed both her palms on his face, and pulled him in for a kiss. When she pulled away, he stopped her, never taking his eyes off hers.

"When you came back from that plane, whatever it is, I thought you were gone. That I'd lost you. Rue, I don't know what I'd do if that happened. I..." He paused for a second to take a deeper breath. "I love you."

She knew that it likely did not actually happen, but her heart felt like it stopped at that moment. She stared into eyes that looked back at her with such longing and anticipation. He was the only man she wanted for the rest of her life. Ruby reached towards him, wrapping her legs around his waist and leaning in close. Her lips at his ear, almost close enough to bite. "I love you, too." She whispered and pulled him into her.

Whatever Demas had planned didn't matter. Her fears and worries had all but disappeared. They would have time to deal with them tomorrow and for the rest of their lives. That is how much time she was sure they had. The only thing Ruby wanted tonight was more of this. More of Liam and the warmth and safety of his body. She kissed him again, this time without a hurry. She didn't want to rush through this because every single second of it mattered. All Ruby wanted was to remember them this way forever. Crystallized in a night of love and tingling fingers, discovering new territories.

CHAPTER 44
YOUR BIGGEST FAN

Liam's arm draped around her stomach and she watched it moved up and down with her every intake of air. She stroked his hair mindlessly, adjusting her eyes to the dim light falling from the lamp and casting sharp shadows in his room. It must have been well into the morning by now, but Ruby felt like she could still sleep for days.

"Morning." Liam said, and rolled over to his side to face her. His eyes just as tired as hers. "So, how's it going?" he teased.

"I've been better." She laughed.

His hand travelled under the covers, pinching her thigh and making her instantly remember that she still had no clothes on. "Have you now?" He smiled, pinching her again.

"Obviously not. But I could kill for a coffee." She

immediately regretted her word choice. The one thing she knew he didn't want to hear right now was a joke about killing. Alice's death coated every inch of the center and while they still had not talked about it, the effect it had on Liam was as obvious as a fire in a dark forest. "I just meant I'm tired. In a good way."

"Rue, it's okay. You don't have to tiptoe around me."

"Have you thought about it at all?"

He sighed. The longest, most weight bearing sigh she'd ever heard. "I'm trying not to."

"But you know, at some point we'll have to deal with it."

"I know. Today is not that day though."

Ruby wanted to push further. She wanted to pin him down and ask him to tell her exactly what he was thinking. To burrow inside his brain and pick out all of his emotions one by one until they lay on a table for her to fuss over. Instead, she said nothing more. Putting her own feelings aside, she wrapped her legs around him and pulled him in close. Her hands continuing to play with his hair as though nothing had been said before.

The one thing Liam needed right now was an anchor, and she was determined that she would be the one to settle him in the storm.

"Mind if I join?" Cyril's voice startled her in the cafeteria.

She looked at her own reflection in his steel blue eyes trying to see if she looked different this morning. *I definitely should have brushed my hair,* she thought, and pushed the chair next to her out with her leg. "Of course not."

Liam was still showering, taking his sweet time to join her for breakfast, and despite the fact that she did not anticipate nor want Cyril's company, it would be rude to send him away. She shoved almost a handful of eggs into her mouth, hoping to prolong small talk as much as possible.

"Strange having everyone under one roof." He noted, his eyes watching her as she chewed.

"It's safe. That's what matters."

"Right." Cyril sighed and started cutting his omelet, "I see you've brought the human girl here as well."

He was clearly not impressed by her decision. She wondered if he knew about Shaylah and Jake and if he even cared. After the last couple of months, she had a feeling that he would not care much for any girl Jake dated unless they were her. Cyril had a talent for moving his family name up the food chain.

"Is there a problem with that?"

"No, not at all. If you think it's necessary, then she should be here."

"She's my friend and it's safe to assume that

everyone close to me is a target. So yes, I do think it's necessary."

"I'm not trying to make problems, Ruby."

She narrowed her eyes to look at him. What was he up to? She hated talking to him this early in the morning. Especially after the night she had with Liam. If she didn't know any better, she'd wager he was purposefully trying to steal every drop of happiness she had left. "What are you trying to do exactly?"

"Just making conversation."

"Right." Ruby was done with the pretences. If he had something to say, he'd better spit it out. "Most people talk about the weather."

Cyril let out a belly laugh that made her even more furious. She wasn't trying to be funny and she definitely didn't want him to think that they had the type of relationship where they could laugh together.

"I can see you'd rather eat your breakfast in peace," he said. "I was hoping I could ask for a favor."

Oh, this should be good!

"I know it's not my place to ask but I would really appreciate it if you watched over Jake."

Her mouth gaped. She dropped her fork and stared at him, pretending to still be chewing her breakfast. The truth was, if she still had any food in her mouth, she would have been choking on it right about now. "You want me to do what?"

"To take care of him. I know it's a lot to ask but I

figured,.o as his closest friend, you wouldn't mind."

"I don't know if you noticed, but Jake can take care of himself. He's one of our strongest *knights*." Her voice raised at the word in case the center spy was around. Might as well kill two birds with one stone. "Besides, he's not my biggest fan right now."

"He's always your biggest fan, Ruby." He smiled like he knew something she didn't, "Just promise me that if he wants to do something heroic, you'll stop him? He's the only one we..." Cyril paused and lowered his head and for a moment, she thought she saw tears in his eyes. She waited for him to finish the sentence but he took a sip of coffee instead. Vulnerability was never his strong suit.

"Just please promise me you will make sure he keeps his head together. No matter what," he said.

Ruby didn't need to ask what he meant by that. She was the 'what' in that sentence. Cyril had assumed that if it came down to it, Jake would risk his life to save her. She wanted to tell him that he was wrong, that Jake had moved on with Shaylah. But hearing his father this worried about him now made her wonder if he hadn't moved on as quickly as she thought he had. She looked up at Cyril and for the first time saw something they could actually have in common. They both cared deeply for his son.

"Okay. I promise." She said, and continued her breakfast. It was one promise she knew she could keep.

CHAPTER 45
MID PERFORMANCE

The knights were lined up in two neat little rows as she marched them down the hall towards the library. Before they left their training rooms, she had instructed them to make their footsteps as loud and intentional as possible. The more noise they could make and the more attention they garnered, the better chance she had of following through with her plan.

As they marched down the hallway, she could see people slowly come out of their rooms, wondering where the noise was coming from. She smiled at her viewers as they passed, a fake procession for a self-proclaimed queen. If she didn't have to keep this charade going, she'd be on the floor laughing right now.

Ruby's hand toyed with the counterfeit Onyx on her neck. It looked almost identical to the real thing but the weight was off. This one was light and airy and didn't weigh down her emotions like the real thing. She'd worn that necklace for so long that it felt like a part of her was missing now, and she wondered how long it would take for the sword to start calling her again. Having a piece of it around her neck helped tame the visions but she was sure that as soon as the connection was severed, she'd be right back to sweaty nights and fearful mornings. Not that she wasn't full of fear already.

"You think they're buying it?" Liam whispered in her ear as they walked.

She wondered that herself. Right now, while this entire charade was mid-performance, Zag and Leah were moving the remaining pieces to one of the shops two streets down. To a randomly chosen location but close enough to keep an eye on. Her parents offered to keep the pieces in their apartment but she vetoed the idea before they had a chance to finish the sentence. It was bad enough they didn't want to move into the center where she could keep an eye on them, but putting them directly in Demas' path was out of the question.

"They'd sure better," she said, and walked into the library, followed by Liam and Jake.

"So, what do we now?" Jake asked.

She thought about his question. It wasn't such a complicated plan. All they had to do was make it seem like something big was happening. The rest of the knights had already split up and were going to be bringing the elders one at a time to the library in the same false parade they had delivered her. That should buy enough time for Zag and Leah to move the pieces and get back before anyone notices they were gone. Ruby was crossing her fingers in hope that the elders could keep the act up long enough. She had no doubt Cyril and Elena would have no problem staying in character, their icy demeanor rarely gave away anything, as it was. Myriam and Harvey, on the other hand, would need to be completely encased in knights to prevent their loose tongues from spilling information to every smiling face they pass. She touched the Onyx again, disappointed at its lack of power.

"Now, we wait."

CHAPTER 46
SOME CREEPY OLD LIBRARY

A few hours passed before they got a call from Zag and Leah. The drop off point was close and when they hadn't returned in a short time, Ruby immediately worried. She wanted to send the knights out to search for them, but Liam convinced her against it. If they were fine, sending everyone out in a panic would just blow their plan.

Zag sounded excited on the phone, but refused to let them know where they were or why they took so long to get back.

"So, he didn't say anything at all about it?" Liam asked. She could tell he was just as annoyed as she was.

"Nope. Just that he can't talk and that they'll be back soon. It sounded like he was running or something."

"Wow. Must be big. I haven't seen Zag run in years,"

he laughed. "You want a coffee or something? Might be a while until they get here."

The door burst open just as he finished his sentence and Zag ran into the room followed closely by Leah. Ruby didn't get out of the way quickly enough and ended up getting hit square in the face with a handful of his matted, red hair.

"Geez, Zag! Watch out!" She yelped, "Where have you two been, anyway? We thought something happened!"

"You guys are never going to believe what just happened!" Zag threw up his arms, completely disregarding what she just said.

She looked back at Leah, who met her gaze with an eye roll. At least she wasn't the only one who thought his dramatics were unnecessary. "Are you going to tell us or should we start guessing?" She asked sarcastically.

"Picture this! We just dropped off the pieces and were heading back here when I see this dude join a group of other dudes on the corner. They looked totally normal but I just got this feeling like something was off. So, I make Leah hide behind this food truck with me so we could get a closer look." He lowered his body to mimic them hiding, "So, we get closer. Like so close I can almost smell their breath. At this point, Leah thinks I'm nuts so she's pulling me back. But I know something feels off."

"I thought he'd finally lost the last marble in his head," Leah added.

"Yeah, whatevs. Anyway," he continued, emphasizing the word, "I keep trying to see these guys' faces, so I could read their lips or something. And yeah, I know I can't read lips but I was thinking maybe I like magically learned or something. So, I keep waiting for one of them to turn around and bam!" He slapped his hands together so hard that Ruby jumped back from the sound.

Liam, Jake, and two other knights in the room were just as surprised. Until that point, they had been leaning in close to Zag, listening to the story like they were watching a movie. "Bam what, exactly?" One of the knights asked.

"Their eyes! Fully black. No whites, just like Ray had!" His eyebrows moved up and down as if he was saying something clever and sneaky, "Coincidence? I think not!"

"You think they're AetherBorns?" she asked.

"I don't think, girl. I know."

"How many?"

"Four. But there's more."

"Unfortunately," Leah added.

Zag sat on the table next to where Ruby was standing. His eyes as wide as saucers, unable to contain his own excitement. "After that dude looked at me, I thought for sure we were caught! But he had no clue. They started walking away, towards the subway. So, I drag Leah with me, she's still clueless as usual but I motion for her to stay close and keep quiet."

Leah slapped his arm and rolled her eyes again.

"You followed them?"

"Yeah, girl! All the way to Lakeside!"

"Lakeside? That's where we found Ray." She noted, slowly putting the pieces together.

"Bingo! I told Leah we need to stay with these dudes. And we did. All the way to some old, decrepit library that looks like it's been shut down for, like, a hundred years."

"Okay, that's definitely creepy." Jake whispered, still hanging on to every one of Zag's words. His animated features made him quite the natural story teller. Red hair bounced all over as he jumped from spot to spot to bring his tale to life.

"No kidding. We didn't go inside though, 'cause this one here was scared." He pointed at Leah, sticking his tongue out at her as he did.

"Obviously! Have you not seen any movies? I'm not dying in some creepy old library!"

Ruby reached over and squeezed her arm. She wasn't sure what she would have done in their place but she knew this was a good call. They could have been ambushed as soon as they walked in. "That was a good call, Leah."

"Oh, and there's more. We stayed behind for a bit to

see if anyone else showed up and there was at least a dozen more of them that went in."

"Oh, my God," she whispered, "you found their meeting place."

"Looks like it! That's why we couldn't call or nothing. We had to be supes quiet until we were sure they couldn't spot us." He flipped his hair back with a satisfied grin, "So, what now?"

"I need some time to think." Ruby said, "If that's where they all meet, we can ambush them but we'll need a solid plan. And we'll have to make sure that Demas is there when we move in." Liam put his hand on her leg to slow her down. Her heart was racing now and he could see in her face how overwhelmed she was starting to feel. She thought she saw Jake squint his eyes and look away from their show of affection but moved past it.

"What are you thinking of doing?" Leah asked.

"I'm not sure, yet. Give me a moment to go over some options. I know there's a plan but I just can't quite see it, yet."

She paced the room, going over every possible scenario. The last time she agreed to an attack, it didn't exactly play out as she'd planned. She wanted to make sure this time was different. Demas was strong. Stronger than anyone she'd ever met. She didn't know if they could overpower him, so they would need to outsmart him instead.

There would be casualties, this she was sure of, what she needed was a way to minimize those casualties. She hated that she was thinking this way. Accepting the fact that people would die, people she cared about. But Demas had already killed Alice. He would not let anyone get in his way. If she could accept death, she could get ahead of it.

Her thoughts raced for hours. Until every one of the knights left the room and only Liam remained. He sat quietly, his legs raised on the table, rocking the chair back and forth. When she cried in frustration, he stayed silent. Moving only to hold her until she was back in thought and pacing around the table again. No matter how badly he wanted to talk it out with her, he knew there would be no point.

She didn't need him right now.

CHAPTER 47
IN THE LINE OF FIRE

The walls of the library were engorged from the number of people in it. Ruby was finally ready to go over the strategy, and wanted everyone's input. Leader or not, they were a team and she wanted to make sure everyone got a say. The knights stuck together with their respective elders, filling every inch of the room. She felt uneasy looking over at Liam who seemed to be out of place without Alice there. He looked like he was teeter-tottering between stepping up in her place and hiding in the shadows. It never occurred to her before, but with Alice gone, he was the next in line for the elder position. Either him, or his parents, and she knew quite well that the Nars had no desire to fill the role. Abigail had barely left their quarters since Alice died. They had tried to check in on her a few times, but Sebastian was adamant that she needed her rest and was not to be disturbed. It made Ruby realize how different they were from her own parents. Pretences aside, there was no familial connection between the three of them. An odd combination to figure out for someone like Ruby, who was closer to her parents than anyone else. She wondered if that would be different had she grown up in an Elemental upbringing like Liam. She couldn't imagine being this separated from her family, and even though she sometimes wished for them to stop treating her like a child, she was grateful for their constant worrying. At least they'd never run off to Italy and leave her to fend for herself.

"I guess we can get right to the point." She said, when everyone settled down in their spots, "I have a pretty good idea of what we should do with this new information, but I wanted everyone's thoughts on it. If it goes wrong, a lot could be at stake and I don't want anyone feeling pressured into this." Pressured into following her decision to go into a possible war zone is what she was thinking, but bit her tongue.

"What could be so questionable that you're worried about people not stepping up?" Cyril asked, glancing quickly at Jake. His concern for his son was admirable and still quite surprising to her.

"I want to attack the old library. Tonight."

A hush fell over the room. Even the noises in the outside hall seemed to dissipate as though upon command. "This could be our only chance to surprise Demas." She added, unsure if it was them, or herself, that she was trying to convince.

"No one saw Zag and Leah follow them. As far as we know, they have no idea that we know their location." Cyril gave her a pointed look, "If we go in unprepared, we'll be putting everyone in danger. What's the point of rushing this?"

"There were four of them just blocks from where we're sitting right now. We have to assume that they know where the entrances to the center are. From my short run-in with Demas I can tell you he's not letting this go. He needs the other pieces. We might not know why, but we do know that if he gets them, he's putting the sword back together. We can't let a murderer get hold of the sword." *Again.* She added to herself, her gaze trained on Cyril.

"That's assuming they know where we are."

She thought of the possible spy in their midst. Whoever was feeding information to Demas and the AetherBorns could be in this very room. "I think we should always assume that they know everything by now."

"Even if that's the case, how do you know that this Demas will be there tonight? We're going to be risking lives on assumptions."

"Zag said he saw more than a dozen AetherBorns go into the library. Why would so many of them need to gather at one time? It's too risky. Demas wouldn't take a chance unless something big was going on."

"Ruby is right," Liam spoke up, "we can't let him get his hands on the sword. If anyone feels like they don't agree, they're welcome to stay behind. But we need to attack while we still have the element of surprise."

"Have you two thought of a plan of attack?" Harvey asked. His shaky hand clutched Myriam's for support. The Earth house was the least confrontational of all four. She had no doubt the two of them were trying to find a way to resolve this peacefully. But there was no way to do that, and she knew it. Demas would not know the definition of the word 'peace.'

"Actually, yes." She cleared her throat, "I'll go with the knights..."

"And me," Cyril said. "Please, don't argue. I can be of good use."

"Dad! No! You've barely had time to train, and I doubt mom would be okay with this. We have it handled!"

Cyril's back straightened and his mouth turned down at the corners. Ruby remembered this face from when they misbehaved as children. It usually came right before a scolding and resulted with him calling her parents. She could see that Jake was thinking the same thing, his shoulders slumped at the sight of his father's irritation. "I don't believe I was putting that up for a debate," he said.

"Fine! Let's just move on for now," she slapped her thighs dramatically, "we can figure out who comes and who doesn't later."

Jake murmured something under his breath but she let it go. As much as she hated to admit it, Cyril's powers were strong, even without any training. Much stronger than Jake or any knight from their house. And if she was right and he was coming along to protect his son, she could count on him not to hold back when it was time to fight.

"As I was saying, I will go in with... the team. We'll hit after dark. I can use the fog to hide us in the shadows and get us as close as possible to the doors." She stepped closer to the table and unfolded the papers that lay there. "Zag was able to find some images of the library and a couple of old floor plans. We know there are two ways in; the front where the AetherBorns entered and the back doors. I think it's safe to assume that both of those will be guarded."

"So, how do we get inside?"

"We use this window," her finger circled a photograph, forming an imaginary line around a window. "I go in first, then the rest will follow one by one."

Liam looked unimpressed. She was putting herself in danger again and he didn't like it. His eyes traced the outline of the window when he finally spoke. "It doesn't make sense for you to go first. This guy has a personal vendetta against you, if he sees you, we're done for."

"He won't see me. The window leads to a small closet. I'll be out of sight and far from the main library hall where I believe they will be gathering." She smiled to reassure him of her safety but it came off deflated and false. "Besides, I need to go in first for all of this to work."

"Why? I don't understand why you need to..."

"Because she's going to move through time. Aren't you, Ruby?" Myriam asked.

"Yes. That's the plan. I need to feel in danger in order to do that. It's the only way I can use the power for now."

"You'll be completely unprotected. I don't like it." He was not backing down.

"That's the point. Otherwise it won't work. If you're there, I'll know you'll save me and I won't be able to tap in. I only need to stay long enough to see as far as a few minutes in."

"What are a few minutes going to do?"

"They'll show me who's inside and how many of them are there."

She could see him run through the plan in his head. He might not have liked putting her in danger but there was no denying it was the only way for them to find out what was going on before the ambush. It was a good plan and he knew it.

"We'll have to move fast," she added. "If Demas

senses something is wrong it won't be long until he finds us."

"How long do you think we have?"

"I don't know, so once we're in, we have to make it count." Her fingers traced along the floor plans as she explained the fastest way to get to the main library hall. She made sure to retrace the steps a few times. They couldn't afford any mistakes tonight. "Oh, and there's one more thing, I don't want any deaths tonight."

"What? How are we supposed to protect ourselves?" Jake exclaimed.

"There're plenty of ways you can do that without killing." She answered without hesitation but a part of her wondered if she could stay true to her own request. She supposed tonight she'd find out what kind of leader she was willing to be.

CHAPTER 48

LEAD US TO VICTORY

etting ready for the night was much more difficult than Ruby hoped for. Her knee bounced as she perched on top of Liam's work table, making it a center point of micro seismic activity. She felt ready, but the uneven beats of her heart spoke otherwise. Maybe Cyril was right and this was too rushed.

"What if I'm leading us to slaughter?" she asked Liam.

He was still going over the floor plans of the old library, trying to find a way to get everyone in and out even faster. "What if you lead us to victory?"

His matter of fact way of answering should have calmed her nerves but all it did was put more pressure on her. When she originally decided to attack the old library, she was quite certain that it would go over smoothly. Sitting here now, and going over the plan time and again, she realized that she was so hellbent on besting Demas that she hadn't stopped to think about what it might cost them if they lost. All she'd thought about was revenge for Alice. And a little bit for Ray.

"We need to at least acknowledge the fact that we still don't know who the spy is. It could literally be anyone!"

"And?"

"And they could have overheard the entire plan. For all we know, Myriam's the spy!"

"You think Myriam is a spy for the AetherBorns?" he laughed.

"Okay, no, obviously not her. But I'm just saying that our entire play could be blown just because someone switched sides and ran their mouth."

"It could be, yes. But it also might not be. You said it yourself, whatever they're planning, they need the sword. As far as they know, the last piece is still around your neck. If things go sideways, we can use that to our advantage."

She couldn't believe what she was hearing. Was he actually suggesting to use her as bait? The guy who worried if she crossed the street without looking twice? "Liam, that's perfect!" She yelped, "If something goes wrong, I'll just distract Demas with the necklace so the rest of you can escape!"

"That is not at all what I was suggesting, and if

you're thinking I'd let you stay behind waving that thing around like a carrot in front of horse, then you're delusional."

"Worth a shot, I guess," she smirked.

"Look, I know that you have no problem with using yourself as a human shield, but you need to understand that you're important now. You need to outlive the soldiers, Rue. That's just how it works."

"I get to decide how it'll work for me, thank you. And I am an AetherBorn shield if anything."

"Please, just don't do anything stupid tonight." He smiled, "I kind of need you to stick around for a while."

His smile was intoxicating, sending shivers down her spine and curling her toes. She had no idea how she got so lucky. A few months ago, Ruby would never have imagined that someone like Liam would want her. Let alone devote his life to her as he has. She wrapped her arms around him, fitting herself tightly against his chest. "And why's that?" She asked, her lips a sly smile.

"Because I love you, despite your arrogant stubbornness."

His hands moved around her waist, caressing the arch of her lower back, making her skin flush. She lifted up on her toes, reaching for his lips hungrily, letting him be her shield for once and making her forget for just a moment what was coming. She closed her eyes, wishing for a different life. A normal life without the madness that surrounded her. But this was the life she chose, no one forced her down this path, at least not directly. She chose to be here right now, to protect and lead them all. She chose Liam and she wouldn't walk away from that choice, no matter what.

They were lost in their love for what seemed like hours. Pulling away only to breathe and swallow. Both of them wanted to prolong this part of the night and avoid the next. They would have hidden in this room forever if it wasn't for that dreaded knock on the door. Leah was waiting outside to take them to the front hall.

It was time to go.

CHAPTER 49
THE WEIGHT OF METAL

The sun had set by the time they arrived at Lakeside. Darkness covered them, concealing their quiet steps as they inched towards the old library. Having lived in the bustle of Westerlake for years, Ruby had forgotten the silence that envelops the world outside of the city. Her every step felt like an explosion of sound and she wished she had practiced her footing more. She was sure that if Demas didn't know they were coming for him, the clumsy bang of her walking was bound to give them away. Or maybe she was just letting her paranoia guide her.

She shook off her fears and looked back at the small army behind her. A mix of emotions painted their faces in the dark. They were here because she'd convinced them that they would not fail, but Cyril's questions left insecurities in her that couldn't be addressed in the short amount of time they had to prepare for tonight.

They walked in unison down the shadow-covered street. The library was just a few blocks away, sitting in darkness on the edge of town. The light from the last house they passed was barely visible now and Ruby was grateful for the privacy. Whatever was going to happen tonight, at least there were no humans around to witness the spectacle. Although that also meant that if things went wrong, they were entirely on their own.

With each step, they moved farther away from the streetlamp lit path and deeper into the darkness. The only thing that gave off any light was the occasional beam of an Elemental stone on the knights, glowing brighter with shifts of their emotions. She wondered what they were feeling, to make their stones shine brighter. Were they excited? Scared? At this point, she was hoping it was both. At least if they were somewhat afraid, there was a chance they wouldn't make any dumb decisions. Alice's death sent a wash of retribution over everyone in the center and she had no doubt that the knights were here partially out of respect for her. Her eyes caught a glimpse of Liam, glad he was here to keep them in check and focused.

Ruby slowed her pace when they were in view of the library. She gestured for the knights to stop behind her, scanning the area around them. It was quiet. *Too quiet*, she thought.

Her fog encircled them in night as they made their way around the back of the building. There were no lights on but she'd anticipated as much. Demas would be an idiot to draw attention to the library. As they tiptoed past the front door, she caught sight of a sliver of light coming from the window of the main hall. A sigh of relief trapped itself in her throat. Her assumptions were correct, the AetherBorns were gathered in the hall as she'd anticipated, which meant the window they planned to enter through would be abandoned. Could they actually pull this off? She smiled at the thought and kept walking.

"Is everyone ready?" She whispered, when she was sure they couldn't be heard.

Liam looked around, nodding towards Jake and Cyril who returned the approval. "We're good to go."

"No matter what," she continued, "we stick to the plan. I go in alone and no one is to move until I come back out with information."

Liam's face tensed but he stepped aside to let her get closer to the window. She touched the bottom ledge, running her finger across the window frame until she felt the outline of a handle. Her shallow breath stopped as she lifted the glass slowly, trying to silence any sound the worn-out hinges might make. When she was sure the pane was locked in place, she looked back at Liam. Her lips turned up into a smile as she slipped inside.

THE CLOSET WAS SMALLER than she imagined it. Shelves on either side that were crammed with dusty boxes and expired cleaning products. Her nose itched and she was stifling a sneeze as best she could.

Somehow it was even darker here than outside. Her eyes were trying to adjust to the lack of light, but until then, she used her hands to guide her through, making sure she didn't accidentally trip on something and give herself away. When she was certain it was mostly safe, she pressed her ear against the door opposite the window. Nothing. Ruby lowered her hands to her side in concentration. So far, she'd only been able to travel forward with the sword guiding her way. Her entire plan for tonight rested on being able to connect to the future without it, and she was praying that she was strong enough to do that. She slowed down her breathing, inhaling deeply through her nose and slowly pushing the air out, rooting it deep within her. Her mind wanted to race but she steadied it. Concentrating only on the sword, imagining it in her hands again. Even with her eyes closed, she could feel the room fill with fog. The dark getting even darker, thick with her power. Her hands balled into fists and her heartbeat slowed as time shifted around her. She kept her mind on the vision, fast forwarding through it as though it was a movie recording.

In her vision, she floated through the library. Her memory filling with the layout of the halls and rooms. She pushed through, moving faster now and into the main hall. She gasped, a fear of discovery flashing through her. Forgetting for a second that none of this was real. But it felt just like she was there, in the open hall of the old library, surrounded by shelves of books and what looked like almost a hundred AetherBorns. *This can't be right,* she thought. Trying to count the dark figures and hoping she was wrong. *How can there be so many of them?*

Her eyes landed on Demas, standing at the front of the room. His lips were moving, he was whispering something she couldn't quite hear. The words echoed through the crowd of AetherBorns. They were chanting along with him.

What the hell is happening?

She tried to read his lips when something caught her eye, a sparkle in the midst of a sea of AetherBorns. Ruby floated through the black fog-covered figures trying to get closer to where she saw the light. Her eyes widened in horror.

It wasn't a light, just the reflection of metal. Of metal chains. Thick, unforgiving chains clasped around the arms and legs of some of the AetherBorns.

She could feel the weight of metal as though it was around her own wrists. It was the same metal that forged the sword, she was sure of it. The same metal chains that held her in her apartment not so long ago.

How did Demas get his hands on these? She thought. And why?

Floating through, she could see not all the Aether-Borns were imprisoned. There was a large group in the front row that stood freely. Their eyes were black, staring ahead at Demas as though they were in a trance. Their hands were open, reaching back like they were clutching something behind them. There were light groans coming from the back of the room. Pained sounds of AetherBorns weakening.

They're using their power!

The realization hit her like a car crash, knocking her back into the closet and forcing her eyes open. Whatever Demas had planned for tonight, he needed all the AetherBorn power he could gather. She had no idea how he managed to find this many AetherBorns, but one thing was certain, they weren't there by choice.

She rushed back to the open window. Her plan was useless now. This was no longer an attack on Demas.

It was a rescue mission.

"**W**hat do you mean they're chained?" Jake whispered, when she finished explaining what she saw. "That doesn't even make sense."

"I know. But it's what I saw. It was like Demas was using them to power himself up."

"And you said there's, what? A hundred of them?"

"More or less. I didn't exactly have time for roll call."

They were huddled outside the closet window and even though she knew they needed to be quiet, she wanted to yell at Jake to get him to keep up. "Look, we don't have time to go back and forth on this right now. These people need our help."

"What do you want to do?" Liam asked. His hand rested around her waist. "We can't attack like we wanted to, we're way outnumbered. Even not counting the AetherBorns that are held against their will, it still sounds like there are too many of them."

"This isn't about Demas anymore," she said. "We need to help them. We can't just leave them there, getting their powers sucked dry for some creepy plan he has."

"We need to leave." Cyril's voice was almost loud enough to get them caught. He tugged at Jake's arm but to her surprise, Jake didn't budge.

"We do what Ruby says." He said, "So, what's the new plan?"

She cleared her throat, a little thrown off by his rejection of his father. "I think the original plan was good, but we need to alter it. We need to split up. Form three groups. There should be an Elemental from all the houses in each of the groups in case they get caught. It'll be a better chance of fighting them off with a full set of powers. Jake you take one group, Cyril can go with the next and Zag will lead the third." She was trying to avoid Cyril's daggered look in her direction. "Liam and I will go ahead. When I was in the vision, there was a door close to where Demas was standing. We'll go around and try to get behind him through there. We'll keep him occupied while the rest of you free the AetherBorns."

"No way. That's too dangerous. He could kill you right there and then!" Jake said through clenched teeth.

"He won't. Something about me annoys him, last time he wanted to hurt me but he didn't want to kill me. Trust me, if he did, I'd be dead." She tried to smile, "Plus, I'm taking Liam. So, there's that."

She could see that Jake was not pleased with her answer but he was not about to start an argument in front of everyone. They were running out of time and he knew it. He walked over to the window ledge, directing the knights in his group to follow. His eyes looked over at Liam then back to her. Something was different about him this time. They harbored none of the loathing that was there after she rejected him, only pain and concern.

"After you," he said, holding out his hand to her.

THEY CRAWLED through the window one by one, leaving their fears behind as they entered the library. Ruby's persistence was infectious and every step she took forward gave hope to the knights who walked at her side.

Communicating only with hand signals, she motioned for the groups to split up. Jake watched her carefully before leading his group down the dark hall-way. When she was certain they were all safe and out of sight, she grabbed Liam's hand and led him in the oppo-site direction. The hallways worked around the central room where Demas and the AetherBorns were located and she knew the door she saw in her vision was just around the corner. As they made their way closer to it, her eyes caught a glimpse of a shadow in a room just opposite the door. She shook her head, squinting her eyes to see clearer. It couldn't be! Her eyes must have been wild from the darkness.

For a second, she was certain that she saw Ray in the room.

Ruby stopped in her tracks, putting her hand on Liam's chest to pause him beside her. She gestured at the room but was met only with his confused face. Her hand pointed at the door, making her fingers trace the motion of walking. He nodded and followed her in. As she made her way inside, she felt sick. Her stomach dropped and the hairs on the back of her neck danced in unison. Something was wrong. The air had a familiar gleam to it and the floor was covered in black fog.

The AetherPlane! She thought but it was too late.

There was a sharp jab at the back of her head. She reached her hand to her scalp and felt an oozing liquid coat her palm. Whether it was blood or black plasma mattered little now. Her hands reached towards Liam, lying unconscious behind her. The last thing she remembered was screaming his name before her eyes gave way, sending her into darkness.

CHAPTER 51
THE SMUG SMILE SHE HAD
BEFORE

Ruby's eyes opened partially, fighting against waking up. Through the slits, she could see they weren't in the hallway anymore. Stacks of bookshelves climbed around her. Some reaching as high as the ceiling. It was brighter where she was now and when she was finally able to open her eyes fully, she realized she was in the main library hall.

Her heartbeat raced no matter how much she tried to calm herself down. She had no recollection of how she ended up in here or how long she'd been asleep. Her back rested on something cold and cylindrical. Probably a table or chair leg. She moved her clammy hands to push herself off the ground and suddenly realized the heaviness around them.

Crap!

Looking down, she realized her hands and legs and

had been chained in the same metal she saw in her visions. The same chains holding the AetherBorns. Her body tensed as she tugged against the weight of her imprisonment. Every time the metal touched her body, her muscles tensed against it. She could feel herself being drained, as though her powers were being sucked out of her body and into the chains.

"Rue!" A familiar voice whispered to her right. She looked over, tears flooding her eyes. He was okay. Tied up just like her, but okay. "Rue, are you all right?" Liam whispered. There was a large gash on his forehead that seeped blood. "Did they hurt you?"

She shifted her body to get a better look at him. There were a few bruises on his arms but the cut seemed to be the worst of it. "I think I'm okay. What the hell happened?"

"They knew we were there. I don't really remember anything. One second, I was following you into that room and then I was out cold. Woke up here with everyone else."

"Everyone else?"

Liam's eyes widened and he gestured behind her with his head. She rearranged her body to get a better look. Her hands went limp in her lap and she slumped her back against the table leg. She looked at the faces of the knights behind her, chained to random parts of the library much like she and Liam. Her eyelids felt hot and tears pooled behind them, ready to flood. They were all caught. Some were still unconscious and some were groggily coming into awareness of what happened. She found Jake in the midst, his head hanging forward onto his chest, arms tied behind his back. Next to him, Cyril's fixed gaze on her made her feel even more hopeless. No one was coming to their rescue now. Her plan might have gotten them all killed.

"Doesn't feel so great being on the other end, does it?"

Her head tilted towards the black boots that stood in front of her. She didn't need to look up to know who it was. She'd recognize Ray's infuriating tone anywhere.

"How?" Was all she could muster as she watched Ray flip purple strands of hair from her face.

"How what? How I'm alive? Or how did you not figure this out earlier?" She smirked. Her smile made Ruby's skin crawl. It would be nothing less than satisfactory to punch this girl straight in the teeth right now. "Did you seriously think we didn't know what you were up to?"

"I..." she had nothing.

"You're an idiot." Ray's smile widened to show a row of perfect teeth, "You should have stopped getting in our way. It's all your fault these dumb Elementals are going to die. Maybe we'll start with the pretty one, see how much you really care about him."

Ruby pushed against the chains to pull herself higher up to Ray's level. "If you touch him, I will kill you!" she yelled, but even she knew how lack-luster that must have sounded. She had no control over this situation. Ray bent down a little to meet her eyes and that's when Ruby saw it. The black veins running from her pitch-black eyes all the way down her face to her neck. The same veins Ruby herself had when she was in the Aether Plane. It was like they were remnants of the place, tainting the blood of everyone who stepped foot there.

"So, that's where you've been," she said, putting it all together. "Hiding in the Aether Plane. You're the spy!"

"God, you're so stupid. All of you. Running around, trying to get ready for some big attack. It was hilarious to watch really." Ray laughed, spitting bits of saliva in her face. "I for sure thought you'd caught me a couple of times, but I guess you're not as observant as you think you are."

Ruby remembered the odd feelings she had of being watched. The remnants of black fog outside Liam's room. Ray had been there the entire time, watching her. And laughing.

"But whose body is in the center?" she asked, if she could just keep this girl talking she could buy herself some time to think of a way to get them out of this. "It looked just like you."

"Did it? I didn't think it was that convincing, but Demas was sure that you wouldn't be able to tell the difference. Guess he was right, you're way too self-absorbed to notice the details." She flipped her hair again, this time hitting Ruby in the face with it. "Die some corpse's hair purple and you saw what you wanted to see. So stupid."

"You killed someone for this?" Her mouth gaped open.

Ray's eyes widened. She seemed taken aback by her assumption, as if she wasn't already working alongside a murderer. "What? No! That chick was already dead when Demas found her. We just got lucky that someone dropped dead that kind of looked like me." She said, but Ruby had a feeling that luck had nothing to do with it.

"Why, Ray? You seem like a good kid. Why would you help him? He's a monster."

Ray stood up straight, squinting her eyes down at her. Her hair hung around her face, concealing most of the black veins. The smug smile she had before was gone now, and all Ruby could see on her face was anger. Anger and hatred. She lifted one of her boots and swiftly brought it down to Ruby's ribs. The kick sent pain all the way down her leg, making her cry out in agony. "You and these disgusting Elementals are the only monsters here."

Ray's hands reached into the back of her boot, pulling out a hidden knife the size of a small hand. She flipped the handle, revealing a blood-soaked blade. Her hands moved quickly and before Ruby could move, the blade was pressed against her throat, digging into her skin.

"I wouldn't be a smart mouth, if I was you. Or the next time I cut your boy-toy I'll make sure to do more damage."

Her eyes pierced through Ruby and she could swear she could see her own reflection in them. They looked like two crystal balls, full of trickery and magic. Ruby nodded in agreement, knowing that if she didn't play along, Ray was certain to start a killing spree.

"Good," Ray said, and pulled her chains to get her to stand, "what do you say we say hi to Demas?"

Ray pushed her away from Liam and the knights towards a sea of chained AetherBorns. As she passed through them, she tried to plead for help with her eyes but her attempts were futile. Most of them were looking down and the ones who managed to meet her gaze projected nothing but fear. The same fear she herself was starting to succumb to.

CHAPTER 52
THIS FAMILY OF YOURS

By the time they reached the front of the room, her wrists were sore from the chains. Ray was not exactly light handed, pulling and pushing her through the crowd like she was nothing but air. Demas stood a few feet away from the first row of AetherBorns, his back turned to them. He was hunching forward, moving his hands in an indistinguishable pattern, strangely illuminated. She could see the light from her vision but something was strange about it. It was as if it was suspended in mid-air somehow. Ruby could only compare what she saw to a crack of light shining through a half open doorway, except there were no doors around. She tried to see past Demas and into the light but there was an emptiness there that she couldn't quite understand. As though what she was looking at was light and dark at the same time.

She felt the same way looking at Demas when he finally turned around to face them.

"Welcome to the party, Ruby." He pushed a ringlet of hair behind his ear and flashed his teeth at her. Smiling did not come naturally to him, he looked like a growling wolf that was trying to grin to keep the sheep from running off. "Too bad it couldn't be under better circumstances."

"What the hell is this?" She bellowed, her arms and legs kicking against the chains, "Why can't you just leave us alone? Why do you ca..." She stopped as her eyes caught a glimmer of light reflecting off something very familiar. The sword. The bastard had the sword.

His eyes followed her gaze to his hands. "Oh, Ruby. You didn't honestly think you could keep me away from something I want, did you?" Another grin, this one was more convincing, and she was certain it was her pain he was laughing at. "There are AetherBorns out there that actually believe in what we're doing here you know. The ones loyal to their heritage."

"You mean like Ray over here? You're getting a kid to do your dirty work for you? Real noble, Demas." She growled.

"I wouldn't underestimate Ray, if I were you. She's been watching you for months, and you've been none the wiser."

"Months?" she asked, wondering how she never noticed her lurking about.

"That's right, dumbass!" Ray brought her boot to the back of her knee causing her to fall to the ground. Her knees hit the cold marble, sending an echo of pain up her thigh. Ray lifted her leg again, ready to kick her down further when Demas interfered.

"Now, now. Let's not break our toys until we're done playing with them." He leaned over with an outstretched hand towards Ruby. "Oh! Silly me! I forgot about the chains." His hand grasped her arm to pull her up gently. "A slight precaution until I can be sure that you're not going to cause any more trouble. I'm sure you understand."

"I don't actually understand any of this. Why do you need me? You already have the sword and your little night light over there," she gestured to the suspended light behind him, "what could you possibly need me for?"

"These Elemental savages don't teach you anything at all, do they?" He looked back at Liam who was still trying to get out of his chains, "The sword chose you, Ruby. You're the only one who can wield it."

"Wield it to do what?"

"To help me power up my little... what did you call it? Nightlight?" He looked back at Ray and both of them smirked. The AetherBorns in the front row were all chuckling under their breaths. It was like they were part of some big joke Ruby wasn't a part of.

"So, what is it?" she asked, genuinely interested in

the answer. She had never seen anything like it. It was an anomaly of conflicting things. A light that was dim, a void, and yet a solid thing that she was sure she could touch. She was mesmerized by it. Too bad it was made to please Demas and was likely pure evil.

As if reading her questioning eyes, Demas walked back towards it, pushing a hand into it. She could see his hand turn black where it touched the illumination, slowly being swallowed in plasmic ooze. When she looked closer, she noticed the air around it shining. Brilliant, diamond-like sparkles. Her eyes widened to the size of small saucers.

The Aether Plane!

"You're finally getting it, Ruby. It's not just stupid a 'nightlight' now, is it?"

"But I don't understand. You brought me to the Aether Plane. All on your own, there was no weird, glowing doorway then. Why this?" She nudged her head at the glow, "Why now?"

"Honestly, you kids, these days really don't know anything about where you came from. It's infuriating." Demas stood beside her. He reached over to brush a lock of hair from her face but she pulled back so fast that she almost fell over backward. She'd take a concussion over his false niceness any day. "The Aether Plane is so much bigger than the place you visited. Think of where you got to go as kind of a perk of being an AetherBorn. A bridge of sorts, one that only you and others like you can access. When you go there, it takes a part of you and you take a part of it. That exchange of energy is what fuels it, what allows it to exist. The farther you travel, the bigger the energy needed, so big it starts to seep out sometimes. Thus..." he waved his arm around the light, "Ta da!"

Ruby's heart rate sped up. The black veins, her eyes, the lack of energy she had lately. All of it lined up with what he was saying. But she couldn't very well trust him. Or could she? "You said bridge. Where does it go exactly?" she asked.

"Ah! Well, that is the brilliant part, isn't it! It goes wherever you need it to go. It is everywhere."

She looked back at Liam and the knights. This was starting to sound like nonsense and she needed to see if they were in any condition to escape. One quick peek stopped her short, Ray was already walking over to Liam, knife in hand. "Get away from him!" she yelled, winning herself nothing but a sly smile from Ray in her direction.

"Don't worry, darling. She won't hurt him. Unless you don't cooperate, of course." Demas pressed two fingers into her chin and spun her head back towards him. "So, what do you say? You'll play nice?"

"What the hell do you want from me?"

"Well, it's very simple. I need the sword. You wield the sword. Therefore, I need you."

"To do what? I don't even know what any of this crap is!"

"To command its power, of course! It's the only thing that will open the gate. The only thing powerful enough."

The gate. The word that kept coming up in her grandmother's journals. Could this be what she wrote about? But how could she know about this? And where did this gate lead?

"Gate?" Ruby asked.

"Like I said. The Aether Plane will take you anywhere you want to go."

"And where do *you* want to go?"

Demas laughed, sending shivers down her arms. The silvery sound of his voice made her push against her chains harder. She couldn't stand to be near him for much longer. "I just want to see my family again." He said, pulling her closer to the light. "It's been a while, you know."

He's insane and there is no arguing with someone like that, she thought. Her best bet was to get everyone else out of here. If she could just keep them safe, she could control him. Or bargain with him. Anything that would make this madman get a grip on reality.

"Let them go, Demas. Let the Elementals and the other AetherBorns go. I'll do whatever you want." She said, and hoped for the best.

"Well, look who came out to play leader after all!"

He yelled so loudly that the back of the room shook, "I guess they weren't all wrong to put you at the top of the food chain! One little problem though," he sneered, "I need all of you."

"What? Why? They can't even use the sword! You said it yourself!"

"No. They can't. But their powers are a good source of energy for when we need to recharge. And trust me, you'll need a pick me up to get this going."

The blood rushed from her face, running down her body and almost escaping through her toes. Her face became ten shades paler than it had been even in the dead of winter. It finally made sense. Why he made sure to keep Liam and the knights alive, the chains around the AetherBorns. This entire library was a prison. Worse, a lab. Pulling energy through the chains and into the next vessel like a blood pump. She had no idea if Demas could drain enough of their powers to kill them, but she wasn't ready to find that out. She needed to get them all out of there immediately. She just needed to play along long enough to figure out her next move. "And if I don't help?"

"Oh, sweetheart. That is entirely up to you, of course! I am not one to take away someone's free will. Especially a family member." He sly grin returned and her stomach turned at the sight of it. "But I would hate for you to regret your decision later. People have been known to go mad after refusing me." His dark eye winked in her direction like he had some secret she didn't get to share in. "Mad enough to hang themselves in their rooms even."

Her breath was gone. Knocked out of her by his words, words that may as well have been a mallet. He was talking about her grandmother. He knew her. Not only did he know her, he was the reason she was dead. How? How can someone make a person hang themselves? It didn't make sense. Ruby tried to slow her panting breaths. She needed to keep talking or she was sure she would either pass out or soil herself. "What did you have to do with her?"

"Lydia? Nothing much. I found her like I found the rest of my children," he pointed at the crowd of Aether-Borns behind them, "afraid and alone. Getting visions of things she couldn't possibly understand. Things she didn't believe in. I offered her a choice the same way I'm offering one to you. She refused."

"So, you killed her?"

"Heavens, no. I simply nudged our little world closer to her. To make sure she understood that we are her real family."

"You threatened her?" She was furious. "What did you do?"

"I showed her that she belonged with me, not that pathetic husband of hers or that little brat she was always coddling." His eyes met Ruby's, "It's not my fault she decided to put on some crazy act and get herself dragged off to an institution."

Ruby's eyes were lakes now as she thought about what her grandmother must have gone through. How alone she must have felt. She was never insane; the visions never drove her away from reality. She knew exactly what she was doing, she gave up her life to protect her family. It was time Ruby took a page out of her book and did the same. "So, where exactly is this family of yours?" She asked, trying to conceal the panic in her voice, "You couldn't just get them airfare or something?"

"Silly girl. My siblings haven't set foot on this pathetic heap of a world since they first created it. Not after they stowed me away in a nice little prison of my own. Making me sit by while your disgusting Elementals ripped apart the only thing in their creation that brought me joy." He ran a skinny finger across her cheek and she shuddered at the touch, "I think it might be time that I repaid their kindness." He spat out the word like it was salt caught between his teeth.

Ruby's head spun. She remembered the stories of the Gods that Alice shared with her. The story of Eirene. Of the birth of AetherBorns. But it couldn't be. If everything that they found in the books was real, that would mean that Demas...

"You're..." she couldn't bring herself to utter the name.

"Oh, yes, of course. How rude of me, all this getting to know each other and I never properly introduced myself. At least not with my birth name." He bowed in front of her in a mocking, theatrical courtesy. "I am Tartarus. It's a pleasure to meet you, Ruby."

CHAPTER 53
ANSWERS

Her eyes danced from Demas to Liam, trying to see if he could hear what was being said from the back of the room. His neck was still flush against Ray's knife but the shocked look on his face told her she wasn't the only one who didn't see this coming. How could Demas be Tartarus? There was nothing in any of the texts that even suggested that there were still any deities around. If she was being completely frank, Ruby still had a hard time believing they were real in the first place. One of the mental notes she'd made for herself when first learning of the origins of Elementals was to find out a more reasonable explanation for how they could possess such majestic powers. If Demas was really who he was claiming to be, how could she even begin to rationalize his existence.

She wanted answers. She wanted proof. She wanted

to run out of the building screaming. Instead, she turned back to the light in front of her and took a deep breath through her mouth. "If you hate your family so much, why not just leave them there? Wherever they are."

"I suppose I could," he paused to think over his answer. She hadn't had the displeasure of spending more time with him, but she had a feeling that Demas would not utter a word unless he had a chance to mull it a million times over. "But you've been to the Aether Plane, at least a part of it. You must admit, it's not exactly the worst place to spend time in. I mean, of course, after a millennium in suspended time, it must get quite cringe worthy. Still, it is bearable and that is not exactly how I want to honor my reprisal. What would the fun be in that?" He laughed. A coarse and booming sound Ruby was certain she never wanted to hear again.

"That's what all of this is? Revenge?" Sweat pooled at the base of her back and she felt sick to her stomach. "All this torture and death and for what? Payback because someone hurt your feelings?" She shouted, hoping her voice did not surrender the fear she really felt. Her eyes caught a glimpse of Liam, begging her not to push forward but she had never been keen on following instructions. "Aren't you supposed to be better than that? Better than us?"

"I never said I was better than you, little girl." His relaxed voice made her even more upset, "I never *wanted* to be better than you. I just wanted to be with *her*."

Demas looked down and for the first time she could see something in his face that wasn't pure rage and evil. He looked almost torn. Like a butterfly born without wings. She knew that feeling well, she often felt it in the years she spent pining after Jake. In that mere second, she almost understood him, felt sad for him even. But that was all it was, a second. His dark eyes shot back to her, on fire with resentment and rage.

"That's the best part of this, don't you see?" He growled, his smile as maniacal as his plan, "If my family wasn't so stubborn, I would have been there to protect her. And if your precious Elementals weren't so austere... Well, you read the rest I'm sure. This way, everyone gets what they deserve!"

"And you get to deliver it. Convenient." She spat out.

Demas tilted his head to the side like a dog trying to understand a command his master had not yet taught to him. His eyes narrowed in perplexity, thinking over her comment. When he walked over to her, she was sure he had no other intention than to break her neck right there and then. Instead, he reached his arm around her, getting closer to her than she preferred. He smelled of ash; an extinguished fire of a man. His hands moved quickly behind her and before she could pull back, the sound of metal hitting tile sounded at her back.

She pulled her hands inward, rubbing her wrists where the chains had left scorching red marks.

"While I am enjoying this little chat, it's time you made yourself useful."

Without thinking, she pushed her hands towards him, shoving him away. Her hands moved in unison, encircling the power in her palms until she was ready to let it go. She moved her hands up, ready to strike but when her eyes landed on the spot where Demas was just standing, it was empty. Before she had a chance to turn around, a skinny arm wrapped around her, holding onto her chin and twisting her to the back of the room. Her eyes pooled as she watched Ray start to slice a deep cut across Liam's throat.

"Stop!" she yelled and to her surprise, Ray stopped.

"If you run, he dies." Demas whispered in her ear. "And if you don't do as I say, the rest of them are next."

She looked back past Liam to where Jake and the knights were chained. Most of them awake now, watching the scene Demas was causing. Jake was trying to say something but she couldn't hear him over her own screaming thoughts. "Aren't you going to kill them anyway?"

"Not necessarily, Ruby." His words were as thick as molasses and she wanted to wipe her ears of them, "You and I could make a pretty good team, you know? I'd be willing to make a trade. If you're interested."

She knew he was lying. The only thing he wanted

was her connection to the sword and as soon as he figured out how to severe that connection, she was as good as dead. The same went for everyone else she cared about. She couldn't be the only one who felt this way. Powerful but stuck. She looked over at the rows of AetherBorns chained at the back. Some were obediently looking away but some were staring directly at her, waiting for her next move. She wondered what Demas promised them to get them to join in his bloodbath. Who did he threaten that they loved?

She had to free them. All of them.

"My knights go free if I do this," she said. "And I want Liam and Jake let go immediately. As a show of good faith."

"Only because I have a soft spot for you," he freed her chin from his hand and stepped back, motioning to Ray who pocketed the knife and begrudgingly released Liam's chains. "Let's get started, shall we?" He smiled, handing her the sword.

The light behind them should have brightened as they walked closer to it but instead, it dimmed and turned into a glowing void. Ruby almost laughed at how appropriate that was for the situation. She was finally in a room full of others like her who could help her feel less alone as an AetherBorn, but they were nothing but pawns in a murderous scheme. A lightness that was tainted by darkness out of her control.

She looked back at Liam, making sure he was free

and far enough away from her. His love for her would only get in the way if he knew what she was about to do. "So, what do I do now?" She asked Demas.

"You breathe. The sword will show you the rest."

Ruby could feel his self-assured, deity smile as she closed her eyes. By the end of this night, she'd wipe that grin off his face one way or another. Her thoughts and emotions were in turmoil, but as soon as both her hands clasped the sword handle, she was at peace. It felt like everything around her had stopped moving, similar to how she felt in the Aether Plane. She gripped the handle tighter, feeling the edges of the stones in it with her thumb. After months of training, her arms were no longer those of the frail little girl who had first held the sword, in Cyril's office. She lifted the sword to the gate light, forcing her every feeling to the tips of her fingers. The sword's blade pulsed with energy, with her own power, and she steadied her stand as black fog encircled her body. Inching closer to the gate that was now growing in size. To her right, Demas was grinning like a kid on Christmas morning, ready to collect his prize.

She could see shadows start move just beyond the light. Oddly shaped creatures, slowly awakening. The gate grew even larger, the opening was big enough to fit a person through. Demas's smile seemed to grow with it. There was a tingling sensation in her fingers, like dancing sparks of energy floating in and out. She looked back into the library hall, the AetherBorns behind them were crouching, wincing from pain. She was sucking the power right out of them.

Now or never! She thought, pulling the sword's blade high towards the ceiling. She only had a brief moment to get ahead of all of this.

Her eyes met Liam's as she whispered, *I'm sorry,* right before she used the handle of the sword to strike the back of Demas's back, pushing him into the lit gate.

CHAPTER 54
MAKE THEM FIGHT

The gate light intensified as it swallowed him whole, like a beast that had just been fed. There was no knowing where in the Aether Plane Demas would be and if she had any chance of following him, she had to do it now.

Fear gripped her every bone, but she fought against it. She had to get him away from the library hall and give Liam a chance to free the imprisoned. If she could keep Demas occupied long enough, they might have a chance of surviving this night after all.

Her small fingers gripped the handle of the sword, it was heavy with power. Power it had stolen from the other AetherBorns in the room, power she now shared with it. She hated holding it, being reminded of the pain it caused them. Maybe if she actually succeeded in stopping Demas tonight, she could make up for some of that pain.

Just like you to mess this up, she thought. *Great start to a family reunion!*

Liam was already starting to rise, he'd be running to stop her any moment now. Ray might have a chance of slowing him down but it wouldn't make much of a difference. If he thought she was in danger, he'd die for her.

She gripped the sword harder, pulling up to stop its edge from dragging on the floor and walked towards the gate.

"Liam! Free them!" She shouted back, one foot already on the other side. "Make them fight!"

The light pulsed against her calf, climbing up her leg, hungry for her to pass through. There was no turning back now. Demas had said the Aether Plane is like a bridge, surrounding every part of existence. She could only hope that the bridge would take her to the same spot it took him. Letting her thoughts land on Demas and using him as a beacon of sorts she stepped into the gate.

Her eyes looked back at Liam, frozen in mid-run. She waved her hand knowing he couldn't see her. It made her feel safer somehow.

Here we go. She smiled and made her way into the unknown.

CHAPTER 55
TOO MANY UNKNOWNS

"Ruby, don't!" Liam yelled after her, but there was no stopping her now. She had a plan and he knew exactly how she got when there was something she felt she had to do.

He started to run towards her, Ray already on his tracks. She must have seen Ruby push Demas in and was coming to his rescue like the dutiful little soldier she was. She closed in on him, but he quickly moved to the left, dodging a group of chained AetherBorns. Ray didn't move out of the way fast enough and was now entangled in a mess of limbs on the floor.

The gate's light brightened and when he looked up to the front of the hall, Ruby was gone.

"Goddammit, Ruby!" He yelled at no one in particular.

His hands grew hot, changing from the color of flesh

to pure fire. With the chains gone, his powers were in his control again. He started to run faster to the gate, if he could just make it there quickly enough...

He pushed his way past kneeling figures, women and girls, all chained in groups around him. As he ran by them, Ruby's last words echoed all around. *Free them. Make them fight.* How could she expect him not to follow her? He would follow her until the end of time if he could. His footsteps slowed, wanting to charge in and save her but knowing that he must yield to her demands. She was his queen after all. His hands ablaze, he turned on his heels, shooting a ball of fire into the crowd.

The AetherBorns screeched in fear, some of them closing their eyes as the fire reached them, waiting to be set alight. To their astonishment, the ball of fire gripped the metal chains, melting the hinges and dropping them to the ground. Their bewildered eyes fell on Liam as if thanking him for their freedom.

"Get the others!" He howled in their direction. His hands were already bright with fury, aiming at another group of prisoners.

Freeing them, his attention drifted to the back of the room, trying to find the knights in the midst of the panic around him. He could see Ray pushing her way through to get to him but two AetherBorns stood in her way, black fog rising around them to attack. This should hold her off for a while.

He ran to the outside edges of the room, pushing

old, dusty books out of the way. The commotion was mainly contained in the center, but from here, there was a direct path towards the knights. He could see Jake struggling to free himself without success. Their eyes met. Jake lifted his hands and with a nod of understanding he pushed a ball of fire at the chains, their burnt remains hitting the floor with a metallic thud.

"Get the others! I'll find Ray!"

Jake moved swiftly, freeing Cyril first. His hands cupped the chains, surrounding them in ice and allowing Cyril to shatter them in one quick move. The two of them moved from knight to knight, reassembling their army.

With the knights free, Liam ran back to where he saw Ray, his eyes taking in the scene unfolding in the library. It was a battlefield in a dome of black fog. He watched as AetherBorns tore each other apart. Ripping through the flesh of others like them, using every power available in their weakened state. He'd never seen anything like it. The library was nothing like their training drills, no one could prepare them for something like this. Up until this point, he thought Ruby to be stronger than anyone he'd met. Now there were over a hundred of her, slicing through one another like knives through butter. It was chaos. He needed to get her back here, she's the only one he could imagine being able to contain this.

But how?

He wasn't even sure if he could follow her into the Aether Plane and even if he did, what exactly would he find there? *Would he* even find her?

There were too many unknowns but the only thing he knew for certain was that he had to get her out of there somehow. Before the AetherBorns destroyed each other. He was almost in front of the gate when a hand grabbed his shoulder, pulling him down on the ground. In one unexpected move, Ray was standing next to him, her leg crushing his windpipe.

He struggled to breathe, his hands grasping at her leg without much success. She was so much stronger than he anticipated. Her hands were clenched into fists, pushed together in front of her chest. Her eyes were closed in concentration, she was channeling power from her hands into her leg, making it clench down on him like a brick wall. With every breath he tried to take, her leg slammed tighter on his neck. His eyesight blurred and his chest tightened in painful gulps of air. If he didn't do something quick, Ray was going to kill him.

Fists tight, he powered up his fire and grabbed onto her leg. Bubbling burns formed under his palms, ripping the fabric of her dark jeans to shreds. But Ray didn't flinch, continuing to push against him. Something about her power was protecting her. He'd seen this in Ruby before, when they were training, like she was in a zone, oblivious to what was happening around her. He needed to break her concentration somehow.

His hands moved under her boot, pushing up just enough to be able to speak. "Ruby!" he whispered, looking in the direction of the gate. If he could make her think that Ruby had come back, he might have a chance of getting the upper hand.

Ray's leg eased up, her hands dropping to her sides. Her eyes followed his gaze, quickly realizing that there was no one at the gate. Not quickly enough.

Liam's legs were already wrapped around her waist by the time she realized it was just a trick, pulling her down to the floor with the force of a hammer. He spun around, flipping her over to her stomach and pulling both her arms behind her to hold her down. She wiggled under his weight but he pressed her down into the floor. He was twice as big as she was, and without the use of her powers, he had her pinned. His lips started to curl into a smile when the hall suddenly darkened. His eyes moved to the gate but there was nothing in front of him. It was as though there was no light there in the first place. He was too late, the gate to the Aether Plane was closed.

Despite still being trapped, Ray let out a chuckle. Her eyes were no longer the plasmic black they were before but all the darkness in them still remained.

"Looks like your little queen is on her own."

CHAPTER 56
YOU

R uby's eyes adjusted to the pitch black around her. With the gate closed, the only thing to light the way was the moonlight shining through the windows. She looked out and grinned in disbelief, even the moon was frozen in its place. At least there was no chance of a cloud covering the light it was providing.

Everything around her stood still and she wondered how much time had passed where Liam was, what she would miss while being here. There was so much she was risking by doing this. What if by the time she came back, it was too late? Worse, what if it wasn't her who returned from the Aether Plane? She was blind to the outside world here, but whatever was happening she hoped Liam and the knights were doing their best in protecting the imprisoned AetherBorns.

She hated not being in control, it felt like she was letting life move on without her. Her thoughts shifted to the deities, Demas's family. Or Tartarus, she still felt awkward calling him that. She couldn't imagine being stuck here for eternity like they had been. Why would anyone choose to live outside of life like this? But what did she know about being a God? Time must mean something very different to someone who could never die.

The space she found herself in was quite narrow. Windows on one side and a hallway stretched long, without an end in sight. It resembled the library hallway in some strange sense, but lacked its defining features. Like it was just the bone structure of what the library was. It was the same with what she saw outside the windows. The world she lived in, just minimized. There were enough details that reminded her of home but it was stripped down to almost nothing. She felt like she had stepped foot in a rough sketch of her own world. This was nothing like the first time she was inside the plane.

Her hand moved across the pane of a window as she walked forward, feeling her fingers glide right through it as it turned to air. As her eyes adjusted to the dimness of the light, she saw a familiar sparkle in the air. Breathing it in, she marched forward, her feet kicking the black fog settling on the ground as she walked.

The repetition of the hallway made her dizzy but

she pushed through, convinced there must be an end in sight. Each window looked the same, an identical copy of the one before it. Same trees, same moon, same paved driveway and nothing else. Ruby was getting sick of the view, no matter how serene and beautiful it was. Her arm was tired from dragging the sword and she was exhausted and hungry, suddenly remembering how long it had been since she last ate. Her stomach rumbled and she wanted nothing more than to rest. To lean against a wall and let it hold her until she was ready to go again. Unfortunately, she was pretty sure that if she leaned against anything in this place, she was bound to crash right through it. Her legs were buckling and just as she was about to slow down, her eyes were distracted by something in the distance. She moved her head from side to side, noticing the moonlight bounce off some-thing in front of her. Something round and metallic.

A door handle!

Excitement and relief poured through her, rushing the energy to her legs, moving them quicker. She ran towards the handle, letting her hands cup it slowly. *You can do this,* she thought. Her mind picturing the solid metal in her hands turning to open. To her surprise, the handle held her weight, allowing her to push her way inside.

"Clever girl. You're getting the hang of this place quite nicely." Demas grinned at her from the center of a circular room.

She gazed around, trying to spot some resemblance to a place she might be familiar with but this room was not based on anything in her world. The large, domed ceiling was intricately carved. Every inch of it covered in symbols that trickled down the walls and into the floor beneath them. The walls themselves were barren except for six tall mirrors, equally spaced around the room. Her eyes studied the reflective surface of the mirror next to her, hoping to see her own reflection inside, but she saw nothing of the sort. Instead, the mirrors looked like a polished black surface, similar to the plasmic ooze that she remembered from her last visit to the plane and from her own wounds. She came closer to the mirror just as the ooze started to move. The shape of two hands stretched out towards her and she jumped back, her heart bouncing all the way into her throat.

"Welcome to the family reunion." Demas howled, letting out a shattering laugh into the room. "Glad you could join us."

Ruby tried to catch her breath as she backed away from the mirror. Her eyes studied the other five in the room. Six mirrors for six deities and all were moving except one. The one Demas must have escaped from. "You..." She choked out, "You tricked me! You knew I'd push you in to save them. This was never about getting them out, you wanted in. Why?"

His eyes moved down her body, landing on the

sword. "This?" She raised the sword above her head. "This is what you wanted?" she bellowed.

"Well, of course." His eyes met hers, "There's only one little problem."

"What's that?"

His palm shot out from his hip, pushing out a ray of plasma that formed into the shape of a knife mid-air. The blade grazed the side of her face, slicing her cheek and knocking her down on the ground. "You," he answered and charged towards her.

CHAPTER 57
KNEEL BEFORE THE QUEEN

A spear formed itself in his hand as he ran towards her. He shifted his weight, throwing his arm forward and letting it pierce through the air, rushing directly at her head. She pushed away from the ground, rolling over to her side. The spear hit the wall behind her, exploding into plasma on impact. She didn't waste a minute, jumping up to her feet and moving away from Demas. Her hands worked quickly, forming the plasma into the first thing that came to her mind. She pointed the gun at his chest, pulling the sticky black trigger. There was no sound as the bullet left the chamber. He was fast but not fast enough to dodge a bullet. It hit his shoulder, sending its poison into his body. Wincing from the pain, he rubbed the plasmic ooze off his torn shirt. "You can't win this, Ruby. I need that sword and you're in my way!"

It all made sense now. Demas had no intention of letting her live. Getting her to join his side was just a distraction to get her here tonight. The sword was a part of her now and the only way for him to yield control of it would be to kill her. If he got his way, the Elementals were as good as dead. The power he would have over them would make him unstoppable. Not to mention the other deities. She had no idea what havoc they'd reap if they got out; judging by their brother's behavior she doubted anything good would come out of it. She couldn't let him win. She would need to survive this somehow.

"So, you'd have me dead like Eirene?" she yelled, trying to distract him.

His eyes flickered for a moment, as though a memory flashed by them. Whatever that memory was, he shook it off, sending a shot of plasma in her direction. It changed as it flew and by the time it reached her legs, a rope appeared in its place, tying her legs together and knocking her on the ground.

"She died at the hands of an Elemental!" he bellowed, shooting off another rope at her throat.

Ruby caught the rope with her arm just in time, shaking it off on the ground before the poison had a chance to burn her hand. The plasma on her legs was working its way to her skin, burning through her boots like they were nothing more than air. Her hand instinctively reached down to untie it but she pulled away as soon as she touched it, bright red blisters forming on her palm from the burn. She could see him walk toward her, without thinking, she pulled the sword up and in one quick motion sliced through the black rope binding her. It dissipated into a cloud of black fog, leaving no residue behind.

A grin formed on her face. She had something he didn't. A way out.

Demas's hands moved fast, this time out of what she knew must be fear. He pushed his fists together, grounding his power, then shot them forward, letting go of a dozen blades that barreled in her direction. There was no time to hesitate. She wasn't some little girl anymore. She was stronger. She was faster. She was a queen.

Planting her feet firmly, she watched the blades fly towards her. Her hands grasped the sword's handle, swiping it across the knives. One by one, they smoked out upon impact, disappearing from existence. She started to grin but the sharp pain in her side stopped her. She looked down at her stomach that was now oozing a mixture of plasma and blood. She must have missed one of the blades. She wanted to press her palm against the wound but that would not be the best idea. Touching the plasma would only hurt her more.

"Enough games!" she heard him yell out before slicing through her with a dozen more knives.

The pain was unbearable. She felt as if her skin was

boiling, there was plasma everywhere. And where there wasn't plasma, there was blood. It covered almost every inch of her upper body. Her knees buckled beneath her weight, and she dropped to the ground. *He will not end me!* She thought, using the sword to keep her balance. She could see him working to send more blades in her direction, to finish her off. Her body was screaming as the plasma worked its way inside her but her mind remained unwavering. She thought of Alice giving up her life for their cause. Of the chained AetherBorns, of Liam. Closing her eyes, her thoughts connected to the sword, lighting up every one of the five stones on its handle. She could feel its power intertwine with hers, they belonged to each other now. Ruby raised the sword's blade just as the knives closed in on her.

She expected to be hit again, for more of her skin to be sliced by their burning steel. But nothing happened.

Her eyes opened. Slightly at first then wide with awe. The knives hovered in the air in front of her, as if afraid to approach. In the background, she could see Demas gasp. Something was different. But what? She looked back at the knives but before her eyes could reach them, something caught her attention in one of the mirrors. The plasma that was forming its surface stretched towards her kneeling body. In fact, each and every mirror in the room was pulling into her. Forming some sort of black shield around her and sword. *The deities! I'm using their power!*

Pulling one leg up slowly, then the other, she staggered to her feet. Energy pulsated around her in a way she'd never felt before. She breathed it in, using it to ground her, feeling every single cell in her body become stronger. She pictured sharp, dagger-like points and as if on command, the shield manifested them. Ruby stood taller, surrounded by what could only be described as a plasmic porcupine. Her smile widened as she sent the needles at Demas.

He tried to move out of the way but there were too many of them. The needles stabbed his body from every angle, causing what Ruby could imagine to be excruciating pain. He fell to the ground in a defeated thump. His eyes watched her walk slowly towards him. The shield moving with her every step.

"Didn't you hear? You're supposed to kneel before the queen." She uttered as she raised the sword above her head.

Her arm moved quickly but not as quick as she had hoped. As she brought the blade down, he moved out of the way. The sword connected with flesh, slicing Demas across the cheek with surgical precision. He pushed his palm against it, stopping the blood flow, and ran across the room with Ruby right behind him. She started to manifest something to hold him, a chain, rope, anything to keep him from running farther.

"Where are you even..." she started to shout behind him but before she could finish, he jumped into the empty mirror, leaving a trail of plasmic ooze on its frame.

Ruby dropped to the ground in exhaustion, her mind racing now and unwilling to stop. The shield dispersed and she was once again surrounded by walls of shiny, black mirrors. Lifeless this time. Wherever Demas had gone, he wasn't here anymore. And neither were the others.

She was on the floor of the Aether Plane, half-dead and very much alone.

CHAPTER 58
FEEL WHAT I FEEL

Almost an hour went by before Ruby was finally able to peel her broken body off the floor. Her face was tear-stained and the mixture of saline and blood made it look like she had covered herself in war paint. She hated crying. Everything about it made her feel weak, but when she finally let herself accept what had just happened, there was no stopping the floods.

Demas escaped. Worse, he is hiding out in the Aether Plane with the rest of the deities, and who knew what they should be expecting next.

Dragging the sword down the hall, she let her trembling legs carry her back to where she originally entered the plane, trailing bloody footsteps behind her. She still did not have the slightest idea of how she was able to open the gate that got them here, relying only on the fact that it had something to do with her own thoughts and intentions. *Hopefully, I can think myself back to Liam.* She wished, afraid to wonder what would happen if she couldn't.

The windows all looked the same and she wasn't really sure exactly where she entered the plane in the first place. She peered down the moonlit hallway, seeing no end in sight. It felt longer somehow than it had before, but that was likely thanks to her weakened state. When she walked as far as her legs would take her, she shakily lifted the sword as high as she could manage. Blood gushed from her wounds from the pressure, staining her shirt that was now more red than grey, but she held on. Her mind was scrambled, twisted like a perfectly wound ball of yarn. She breathed in, tightening her grip, pushing everything out of the way except Liam. Her lips curled into a slight smile as his eyes came into focus. She pictured the green shimmer in them when she kissed him, the way the muscles in his back curved with pleasure under her touch, his messy hair in the morning. She thought of all the things that were hers alone, everything that Demas couldn't cut to pieces if he tried. With a final deep breath in, she pushed her thoughts into the blade.

"Here goes." She whispered, watching the gate's light flicker before her.

When Ruby opened her eyes, they were threatening to stream again. She belted out a laugh of relief, allowing herself this tiny moment of happiness as she looked out into the library hall. It was a bigger mess than how she left it and looked as though she was about to walk back into the middle of a war. AetherBorns killing AetherBorns, black fog and blood shed all around them. And bodies. So many unmoving bodies on the floor.

But that's not what she clung to. She could only focus on one scene in particular, her eyes landing on Liam as soon as she opened them. He was frozen, much like the rest, his hands alight and ready for attack. In front of him stood Ray, her arms stretched out to block his shots. *He's alive!* She sighed, only now starting to take in the rest of the scene.

Just beyond them, Jake and Cyril surrounded a group of AetherBorns, their hands outstretched in either direction, containing the cloaked figures in what looked like pellets of freezing rain. Sharp, razor-like droplets frozen in mid-air. Her gaze shifted to the back of the hall where three Air knights hovered over four crouching girls, all grasping their throats, trying to breathe. She could see a large rock wall had been formed down the center of the room, beyond it was a blood bath. Groups of AetherBorns were using every power imaginable to wipe out knight and AetherBorn alike.

It was torture.

Sword still in hand, she pushed herself through the

gate, taking in a deep breath as she walked through, getting ready for what she was about to hear. For the screams. They rang in her ears like out of tune violins, screeching and beyond repair. Damaging her ear drums with their agony. This had to stop. She had to stop them.

"Stop!" she yelled, but not one person heard her. "Stop this, right now!"

Nothing.

Not even Liam could hear her over the sound of their powers crashing into each other.

Ruby planted her feet firmly; she wasn't about to die in the middle of a war led by a coward who ran off the first chance he got. And she definitely was not going to let her friends die in it. Her blood-soaked sleeve shook as she raised her blade, summoning every power she stole from the deities in the Aether Plane. The sword's stones pulsated light, reaching into her mind, hungry for instruction. She thought of silence, of piercing drops of pain to get their attention. *Feel what I feel,* she thought, letting the droplets of black molasses hit their skin as burning plasma rained upon them.

They were unaware at first, so preoccupied with their own mutual destruction to even notice. But then, one by one, they swatted at their skin where the rain hit it. Shielding their eyes while looking up, trying to find out where it was coming from. The rain had silenced them all. So much so that the entire hall could hear the metal clank of the sword as it hit the ground.

"I said, stop." She whispered, entirely defeated now.

Liam bolted to her side, but he was too late. Despite the lack of blood, her body was still heavy enough to drop like an anchor. She hit the tile floor with her shoulder, sounding off a crack that made even Ray's face twitch. He gathered her up in his arms, yelling her name, but it sounded distorted, like she wasn't really hearing him at all. Her head dropped to the side; her blurred vision could barely make out Jake's shape running towards them.

"They have to stop; this isn't the way." She slurred, letting the library hall go black.

CHAPTER 59
YOU WILL ALWAYS HAVE A CHOICE

Liam and Jake fussed around her as she dropped in and out of consciousness. She could hear them yelling orders to others, asking for water and articles of clothing. At one point, one of them carefully took her torn shirt off and she yelped from the pain, her eyes bulging widely before she drifted back to sleep. Ruby jarred back to reality from her slumber to find an AetherBorn she hadn't seen before wiping one of her wounds. The girl called out for Liam but before he could get to her side, she was back asleep.

She wasn't sure how long this cycle continued. When she finally opened her eyes fully, she found herself on one of the library tables in a familiar oversized sweatshirt. Liam's smell still lingered on the collar and she inhaled it as she sat up, treasuring every breath like it was her last. The sleeves of the shirt hung loose around her thin arms, making it easier to lift it up to inspect the wounds. She could see the scars from the cuts all over her upper body as she checked, some were still healing but some looked as though they had been closed for years. They had done a pretty good job cleaning her up.

Jumping off the table, her feet made almost no sound as she landed on the floor, making her quickly realize that she wasn't wearing her sneakers, or pants for that matter. Ruby stretched the sweatshirt as low as it would go and started to walk in the direction of the crowd at the back of the hall. Her legs were still weak and each step took some work but she was determined not to look any more bedraggled than she felt. When she spotted Liam talking to Jake and another knight, she picked up her pace. "Hey, stranger." she said, her voice hoarse and almost non-existent.

His head spun around in her direction, running to her as though they had been parted for years. Wrapping his arms around her, he pulled her up a few inches off the ground, his lips on hers. Her tense muscles eased at his touch and she ran her fingers through his messy hair, catching on her fingertips every bead of sweat from his fight. The room felt empty for a moment but her eyes glimpsed something at the back of the hall, pushing her attention away from him and back to the library.

The door from which they originally entered was

barricaded. A pile of earth and rock covered the wall all the way to the ceiling, making it impossible for anyone to leave. Four knights stood in front of it, legs planted firmly on the ground. A threat to anyone thinking of leaving.

"I see Zag has been busy." She nodded at the barrier.

"Right." Liam slowly lowered her back to the ground, "We weren't sure when you'd wake up. The knights thought it best to contain everyone until we figure out what to do."

"The knights or Cyril?" She asked, not really waiting for an answer. Now that her strength was somewhat restored, she started to see the reality to which she had come back. Fear coated the library hall. There were two large groups of AetherBorns on either side, the captors and the captives, she assumed. She tried to find Ray in the mess of people but her purple hair was nowhere in sight. Ruby had no doubt the crafty scoundrel ran off long ago. Knights watched each group like hungry wolves guarding their meals, with Cyril walking around to check in on them periodically. He eyed her cautiously, like he knew she'd be unhappy with his choice of imprisonment. This was just like him, take any chance to act on fear. Ruby had forgiven him some of his past choices because she cared so deeply for his son, but this wasn't something she would play along with. She couldn't stand the sight of this division.

Running her fingers across the scars on her arms, she pushed away from Liam and marched to the back of the hall.

"This is what I almost died for?" Her voice boomed through the room, "So you could become exactly what Demas thought of you?"

"Ruby, please, we just thought..." Cyril objected, but she threw a gust of wind, sliding him across the floor and away from the AetherBorns before he could finish.

"You thought you could use this to your advantage. Exercise your power while you still had fear on your side! You coward!"

She could see Jake rush to his father's side to help him up, his eyes never leaving her. She could all but smell the terror on him, on everyone in the room. They huddled closer together, even the knights took a few steps back. They were afraid of her, of what she might do, of what she had become. "Just breathe, Rue." Liam's hand touched her lightly on the shoulder and she relaxed into it. "Show them what they can be."

He was right. There was only one way to make them see her point of view. She couldn't force it down their throats even if she wanted to. Even if they were acting like children. She would never become like Cyril, reigning over them with an iron fist. They had to decide for themselves. The turmoil in her subsided, she pushed it deep down until it was nothing but a tight ball of anger. She used that ball to guide her hands towards the stone wall, parting it open to reveal the door behind. Her eyes roamed the room, trying to connect with every AetherBorn and Elemental in it.

"You are not prisoners here." She spoke, her voice quiet and trembling at first. "You can leave whenever you choose, no one will stand in your way. You have my word on this." Raising her voice, a little, she continued, "Demas was a liar. He lied to all of you. Promising some better future based on his own revenge for what was done to him in the past. Using you to fight his battles for him. To right the wrongs of something that happened long before you were even born. I will not be like him. I will not be like those that came before me." Her eyes caught Cyril's but he looked away, ashamed, "you get to decide. You can leave here, go back to the life you had before all of this happened. Forget about tonight, about Demas and about me. Or you can stay. You can help me build something new. A different kind of family, one that all of your ancestors would not have approved of. Hell, one they would have wiped off the face of the world if they could. The kind of family I think is worth fighting for.

"You get to choose what you want tonight, no one else will choose it for you. But if you plan on staying, know it will not be easy. It will be the opposite of easy. There will be more wars, more hatred, more ignorance. There will be more bloodshed." She looked around the remnants of the fight around her, "I can only promise you one thing tonight, with everything that I have, and on my own life. If you decide to stay, you will always have a choice. No questions asked."

The hall was silent but for the shuffle of a few feet. She watched as a couple of girls got up quietly and left the room, their hands balled in fists for protection. Two of her own knights followed them out, leaving an empty pit of failure in Ruby's stomach. When a girl of no more than sixteen climbed to her feet, she was certain she would lose them all, one by one. To her surprise, the girl didn't make a beeline for the door like the rest. She simply stood; her hand outstretched in front of her. Ruby peered into her eyes, trying to understand why she wasn't moving. The girl smiled and nodded her head to the orb of black fog forming in her palm.

Ruby watched, bewildered as the orb grew in size, lifting up towards the ceiling. The girl stood there smiling and waiting. It only took a second for another AetherBorn to join her, throwing her own orb to meet the first one. One by one, they stood and one by one, the air above her filled with black fog. Soon, some of the knights created their own orbs in whatever element they controlled, tossing them into the air with ease.

They're staying. She sighed in relief, watching the library fill with powers. Her body trembled with her laughter. The unhealed wounds staining Liam's sweatshirt with each shake of her shoulders.

Her fingers touched something cold and she looked

down to see Liam push the edge of the sword's handle into her hand. She gripped it tightly, leaning her shoulder on his and letting herself understand what laid itself out before them. Ruby asked them to make a choice and they did.

They chose her.

CHAPTER 60
A NEW LIFE

R uby was a ball of nerves this morning. She stood at the bottom of the staircase in the center's entrance fidgeting with the sleeves of her jacket. Her body was mostly healed from the night at the library but there were scars running up and down her arms that refused to disappear. A parting present from Demas to remind her of him.

The energy buzzed in the center as the Elementals trickled in. They were eager, she could see it in their faces, some even scared, despite the fact that she assured them that this was a step forward. When they returned that night, she was expecting push back from the rest of the group for her decision to bring the AetherBorns in, but even the elders bit their tongue. It was as if she had earned her stripes with them. Not that she was all that surprised, there were no medals on her jacket but the story of her defeat of Demas travelled fast. Leah had still not stopped asking her eager questions about every detail. She wished she could offer her more than just a distorted version of the truth, but there were some parts of that night that needed to remain hidden. At least until she and Liam could understand the danger they might be in if Demas chose to return.

She tugged at her sleeve again and turned to look at him. He looked more stoic somehow, now that he was accepted as the Fire elder to replace Alice. She wondered what that meant for the two of them, how things would change in the near future when it was not just *her* safety he had to worry about. His hair fell in his eyes and he brushed it out quickly, throwing a wink in her direction before continuing his conversation with some of the knights next to him. There were nine of them left, after Liam joined the elders, and the other two deserting the night of the attack. Not a large number, but one Ruby was happy to have on board. At least she knew she could trust the soldiers that chose to stay by her side.

"You ready, Fish?" Shaylah's sharp tone woke her up.

Standing next to Jake, she looked almost like an Elemental herself. She certainly had the dramatic flair for it. It came as a surprise to Ruby that Cyril was in awe of her, even Jake's affections fell flat against his constant drooling over her friend. She wondered how much of the act he was putting on was real, not long ago he'd treated her in a similar fashion. Now he avoided her like the plague; on several occasions actually leaving a room that she occupied. Something Ruby knew she'd have to fix sooner or later. Even with Liam moving in with her and Shaylah, she still spent a lot of time at the center and the last thing she needed was odd behavior from one of the elders.

"Sort of. It's kind of a big deal, huh?" she smiled at her bright-eyed friend.

"Kinda? You're kidding, right? This is huge! At least from what Jake told me." She could see her search for Jake's eyes but his attention was elsewhere, "So, how many are coming?"

"Not sure. We didn't take count or anything. But should be at least fifty, if not more. A lot."

More than she knew what to do with is what she wanted to say, but kept her mouth shut. Ruby had no idea how all of this would play out. She had promised them a new life, a family, something to look forward to, but she still didn't know if that was something she could deliver. It had been decades since the Elementals had to coexist with AetherBorns, let alone this many of them. There was so much to figure out. Why did they all awaken? Did the sword call to all of them? And if it did, why?

There were so many questions that she wanted to find answers to, questions that scared her half to death.

Reminded her of how much rested on her shoulders now, how many people she had to protect. She should have killed Demas when she'd had a chance, but he was too fast for her. What's to say he wouldn't come back even stronger? And worse, with backup?

She felt Liam's lips on the back of her neck, his warm breath trickled down her spine leaving a silent shudder trapped in her throat. He wrapped his hands around her waist, pressing his chest into her back. "Here goes nothing," he whispered, as the door at the top of the stairs slid open.

Ruby looked up with anticipation, pushing every worry away for the time being. Her back straightened and she stood unwavering as the AetherBorns made their descent into the center. A queen welcoming new subjects into her court.

EPILOGUE

Her body shook from the cold, the tiny hairs around her scars were standing up and she rubbed the skin of her arms back and forth to warm up. Her nightgown was soaked in sweat and her hair was a messy hive of waves, threatening to blind her as she moved. She was still disoriented from waking up to the jarring sound of someone calling her name. Someone she recognized in her sleep but had no intention of ever seeing again.

She had started to get out of bed when she noticed Liam lying beside her. His broad chest's repetitive movement usually put her at ease, but was now unusually steady. Her hand reached over to touch him but as she did, something made her realize that she wasn't in her bed any longer. The sparkle in the air coated her hand, flying around her fingertips as she moved them.

A panic hopped from her stomach, settling eagerly in the back of her throat. How did she wake up in the Aether Plane? Could it be her dreams brought her here? She couldn't remember what she was thinking about in her sleep but as far as she knew, she was never able to pull herself into the plane from dreams alone.

But if it wasn't her dreams then it could only be...

"Miss me?" Demas's white teeth lit up from the edge of her bed.

She jumped back in surprise, pulling the covers higher over her exposed legs. His eyes watched her but he didn't move, like he was taking in the sight of her for now. She could see the scar she left him with, running down his face, and couldn't help but smile from the sight of it. "What the hell do you want?"

"Tsk, tsk, tsk. You didn't think you could get rid of me so easily, did you darling?" He leaned forward, making her push herself farther back into her pillow. "I've been around for a little while you know, kind of hard to get rid of."

"Like a cockroach." She said, eyes blazing with anger.

His laugh rang through the plane, sending sparkles of air flying towards her. She imagined that if they were in the outside world, those brilliant points would actually be spit. Her stomach convulsed from the thought. "I heard a little rumor that you have yourself quite the little collection of my children."

"They're not yours. You don't get to claim some-thing just because you share their DNA." She should have been scared, but she was feeling daring, even in her half-dressed state. "You mean nothing to them and they know it."

"Oh, I don't mean any offence, Ruby. I'm quite impressed actually. You're becoming quite the ruler. You almost remind me of her..." His voice trailed off and she knew he was speaking of Eirene.

This guy is delusional, she sat up in bed, getting ready to summon her powers.

"That's what you came for? To tell me that?"

"Relax, darling. No need to get upset. I'm not here to pick a fight with you. Although I would love a rematch of our last soiree. I feel I could do a lot better this time." His hands barely rose in her direction, and a shadow crept over the covers, tightening around her body. She felt the weight of it pulling her down, pushing her hands into the mattress. It was strange that some-thing so light could bear that much weight, but this was the Aether Plane and nothing should come as a surprise to her here.

"Then, what did you come here for? To scare me? You'll have to do a lot better than this."

He thought about her words for a moment. Twirling them around in his mouth like a fine Merlot, tasting them before he shot back with an answer. "Not to scare you, Ruby. Just to warn you."

"Warn me about what? And why?"

Demas raised one finger to his cheek, running it along the scar she gave him. "Let's just say that I've grown bored after so many years here. You've given me a challenge. One I don't want to rush getting through."

Her eyes widened and the sweat on her forehead started to run into them. He was toying with her. Like a cat plays with its food before it rips the throat out of whatever creature it has chosen for dinner. What he made her go through the night of the library was nothing compared to what he was planning on next. He wanted to hurt her and he knew the best way to do that was to hurt the ones she loved. Whatever he was planning, she needed to be very afraid. "So, what's this warning?" she asked, trying to hide the tremor of her voice.

"Quite simple, Ruby." He grinned again, "War is coming for you all. And this time, I'm bringing the right kind of backup."

The shadow slipped away from her and she jumped out of bed. Her hands shot towards him, sending two small arrows in his direction but before they could make contact, the shadow he came with wrapped around him, pulling him out of the plane. She could see the air change, the brilliant light of the sparkle in it disappeared, leaving her sitting on the edge of the bed in the darkness of the room.

"No!" she wailed, punching the mattress in anger.

Liam jumped up in bed, his bare chest now moving

in its usual calm rhythm. Pulling the covers back, he reached over to her, scooping her body into him. "It's okay, Rue. Just a dream." He whispered as he brushed her sweaty hair off her forehead.

"This wasn't some dream." She said, defeated.

"What was it? What happened?"

She looked back at the spot where Demas had been sitting just a minute ago, half expecting him to still be there. Mocking her with his grin. But the room was empty aside from the bend in the covers from where his weight had been. A small reminder of the warning he came to personally deliver. She leaned herself into Liam's chest, opening her mouth ever so slightly, so that only a fraction of the sound escaped.

"War is coming."

THANKS FOR READING!

I would love it if you could leave a short review of the book to let me know what you thought. You can post your review at any of the sites below and I hope you know how much I appreciate you doing this!

https://www.amazon.com/dp/Bo7QMW1ZVD

https://www.goodreads.com/book/show/44824558-aetherqueen

If you want to hear more about my books or be the first to receive news on sales and giveaways, sign up for the newsletter!

https://www.ansage.ca/newsletter-1

A.N. SAGE

AETHERBLOOD

THE AETHERBORN SAGA, BOOK 3

AETHERBLOOD, BOOK 3 OF THE AETHERBORN SAGA

"War is coming."

After barely escaping the AetherPlane with her life, Ruby Black is still haunted by the final words of the ancient being to whom she spoke.

Since that dark day, Elementals have been vanishing, only to show up dead shortly after, killed in the most awful ways imaginable. The bodies have started appearing across the country, and it seems those ominous words might have been prophetic after all. Someone, or something, is systematically wiping out the Elemental race, and if Ruby doesn't act fast, she may soon be a queen of ash and bones.

But catching a killer who is always one step ahead is no easy task; a trap must be laid, but care must be taken or Ruby may find herself walking into an elaborately woven trap herself.

Old enemies arise, and unlikely allies reveal them-selves – darkness is coming, and it will claim all who are unprepared.

No lasting peace was ever achieved without blood being spilt.

BUY ON AMAZON NOW!

https://www.amazon.com/dp/B07V7XB3PT/

ALSO BY A. N. SAGE

Kartgega- Kartega Chronicles Book 1

https://amzn.to/2YFSekp

Kartgega 2.0: A Star Reborn- Kartega Chronicles Book 2

https://amzn.to/2ZhT7yR

AetherBorn- AetherBorn Saga Book 1

https://amzn.to/31tCAdB

AetherBlood- AetherBorn Saga Book 3

https://amzn.to/2VuUxov

AetherWars- AetherBorn Saga Book 4

https://amzn.to/3gcuFWy

AetherBorn- The Complete Saga Box Set

https://amzn.to/3ifXog6

ABOUT THE AUTHOR

A.N. Sage has spent most of her life waiting to meet a witch, vampire, or at least get haunted by a ghost. In between failed seances and many questionable outfit choices, she has developed a keen eye for the extraordinary.

Since chasing the supernatural does not pay the bills, she dabbled in creative entrepreneurship, marketing and retail management. A.N. spends her free time reading and binge-watching television shows in her pajamas.

Currently, she resides in Toronto, Canada with her husband who is not a creature of the night.

A.N. Sage is a Scorpio and a massive advocate of leggings for pants.

For more books and updates:
www.ansage.ca

Connect on social media:
Facebook Group:

https://www.facebook.com/
groups/945090619339423/

Instagram:

instagram.com/a.n.sage/

Twitter:

twitter.com/ANsageWrites

Facebook:

facebook.com/ansagewrites

Pinterest:

pinterest.ca/ansagewrites

Goodreads:

goodreads.com/author/show/
18901100.Alexis_N_Sage

Amazon:

amazon.com/author/a.n.sage

www.ingramcontent.com/pod-product-compliance
Lightning Source LLC
Chambersburg PA
CBHW060226030726
47499CB00004B/1206